BEASTS AND BAKING

Related titles by S. Usher Evans

PRINCESS VIGILANTE
The City of Veils
The Veil of Ashes
The Veil of Trust
The Queen of Veils

THE SEOD CROÍ CHRONICLES
A Quest of Blood and Stone
A Quest of Earth and Magic
A Quest of Sea and Soil
A Quest of Aether and Dust

THE MADION WAR TRILOGY
The Island
The Chasm
The Union

BEASTS AND BAKING

Weary Dragon Inn

BOOK FOUR

S. Usher Evans

Sun's Golden Ray
Publishing

Pensacola, FL

Version Date: 1/3/24
© 2024 S. Usher Evans
ISBN: 978-1945438707

All rights reserved. No portion of this publication may be reproduced, stored in a retrieval system, or transmitted by any means—electronic, mechanical, photocopying, recording, or any other—except for brief quotations in printed reviews, without the prior written permission of the publisher.

Map created by Luke Beaber of Stardust Book Services
Line Editing by Danielle Fine, By Definition Editing

Sun's Golden Ray Publishing
Pensacola, FL
www.sgr-pub.com

For ordering information, please visit
www.sgr-pub.com/orders

Dedication

To H4

Chapter One

"A ladder?" Earl Dollman broke into a wide smile. "Spring *must* be around the corner."

Bev nodded in agreement. While there were still pockets of ice on the ground from the *excessively* snowy winter, the sun was doing its best and a warm breeze was blowing in from the south. Small green buds had appeared on the ground, and some birds had returned. All signs the new season was on the horizon.

Which meant it was time for the Weary Dragon Inn to get its annual deep clean—a feat that required Earl's ladder to reach the second-story windows.

"It's all yours," he said, walking her around the

back of his tidy house to his large workshop. The town carpenter had been busy the past couple of months, what with rebuilding part of the Weary Dragon and a few houses in the aftermath of a spate of sinkholes, then keeping the town's roads clear of *immense* amounts of snow. But the old man, with his pale, bald head encircled by salt-and-pepper hair, hadn't seemed to mind the extra work.

And based on the number of items in his workroom, he'd been busier than Bev had thought.

"Oh, Earl, I hadn't realized you were so good at woodworking." Bev ran her hand along the top of an intricately carved chair. "These are gorgeous."

"Well, it's been somewhat slow, what with all the weather we had around the solstice." He chuckled. "Never been so happy to see a spring in my life." He gave her a sideways look. "Any more… *excitement* over there at the Weary Dragon since then?"

"Not a lick of it," Bev said with a satisfied sigh. "Biscuit and I have been quite happy to have a few weeks of quiet."

In the week leading up to the winter solstice, there'd been a freak snowstorm in town, which had effectively trapped six sets of guests at the Weary Dragon Inn. But more alarming was the mysterious —and threatening—letters the local butchers received. The Witzels thought the "secrets" the blackmailer was going to expose were related to Ida's magical strength, but it turned out the deviant was a military registrar, who'd been traveling the country to blackmail soldiers into giving up gold for his stamp of approval on their official military paperwork.

Bev still wasn't sure how she'd managed to get the Witzels out of that one, and thanked her lucky stars it was the perfidious blackmailer who'd been hauled away in chains, and not her dear friends across the street. Shortly after, the butchers left for a well-deserved vacation to the south.

"Here's the ladder," Earl said, plucking it from against the wall. "It's a bit rickety, but it'll do the job."

"I'll have it back by the end of the day," Bev said, taking it by the wooden rungs. "Should probably look into buying my own, since I come by to ask for it once a year."

Earl shook his head. "Why waste your gold on that when you could just take mine? And please don't be in any hurry to get it back. I don't have much work at the moment, outside of the shop, of course." He gestured to the chairs. "Mayor Hendry's got me working on a pair of chairs for her office, and she wanted them done yesterday, if you ask her."

"And I'm sure they aren't complicated in the least."

"Not at all. Only took a month to get the design

approved by her." He winked. "But anything for our dear mayor. And, uh, the gold she's paying me."

"Well, I can't promise any gold, but I would be happy to bake you a loaf of rosemary bread," Bev said.

"If you insist." He smiled. "You're a star, Bev."

She waved as she hoisted the ladder under her arm. "Likewise."

While she would've liked to have taken her time washing the windows, tasks had a way of piling up if not tended to quickly. Bev's annual cleaning list included scrubbing the rugs, scrubbing, waxing the floors, and deep cleaning her oven and stove, to name a few. But at the end of it, her beloved inn would shine and be ready for another year of welcoming guests.

Bev propped the ladder on the side of the inn next to the front window and headed back toward the water pump. Biscuit, her mischievous laelaps (a magic-detecting creature who looked like a dog), was sunning himself on the back step, but lifted his golden eyes to greet her. He was barely twenty-five pounds (though he seemed to have added a pound or two in his months eating whatever scraps Bev tossed to the floor), with yellow fur, white paws, and a white stripe down his chest.

"Are you going to help me today, or are you going to laze about?" Bev asked, knowing full well the answer.

Beasts and Baking

The dog rolled onto his back for a moment, scratching himself on the ground, before rolling back onto his side and falling asleep.

Bev chuckled. There wasn't much the laelaps could do that didn't revolve around seeking out magical objects, but she could still remind him he was essentially living and eating at the inn for free.

Her pail full, she added a little bit of soap and tossed a few rags in then lugged it to the front, placing the soapy water bin next to the ladder. She pulled one of the sopping wet cloths out of the pail and ascended the ladder carefully, tackling the first window.

"Window washing time again, Bev?"

She stopped, looking down at Ida Witzel. Petite with tawny skin and corkscrew black hair, she had a wide smile that seemed even bigger than the last time Bev had seen her, two weeks ago.

"Well, aren't you a sight for sore eyes?" Bev said, finishing the window and climbing back down. "How was your trip?"

"It was lovely," she said with a deep sigh. "I've never seen my wife so relaxed."

"Was it your first time to the south?" Bev asked.

Ida nodded. "Vellora wouldn't stop by her village, but we did pass by. It seemed lovely, from a distance at least. But we spent a whole week by the ocean. Oh, Bev. It was magnificent. The salt water and the birds and the warm sun." She clasped her hands as she closed her eyes. "I've never felt so peaceful."

"You both deserve it, after the trouble you had at the solstice," Bev said, wiping her hands on her apron before embracing her dear friend. "But you were missed. I think Etheldra would throttle me if I served vegetable barley stew again."

"I'm sure she was fine." Ida rolled her eyes. "There was plenty of rosemary bread to go with it. Seems like a hearty enough meal to me."

"Regardless, I know she'll be happy to get something else this evening," Bev said.

"Well, all we have at the moment is sausage," Ida said. "Haven't yet been in touch with our farmers to let them know we're back. Would that be all right?"

"We won't need too much. Maybe two or three pounds, at most. It's usually just the three of us for dinner these days."

Her soft smile faded. "No…uh…sign of any of our new friends?"

"You mean Flanigan?" Bev shook her head. "Haven't seen the front or back end of a queen's soldier since they left town. Guess they took the winter off, too."

"We saw plenty on the roads down south, don't worry." She laughed, a little nervously. "I'm glad to hear there hasn't been any more trouble for you. Goodness knows you need a break, too."

Beasts and Baking

Bev shrugged. "It's been nice to slow down. But I'm ready for the spring visitors." She paused, looking at the still-dirty windows. "Well, almost."

"I'll let you get back to it," Ida said with a smile as she turned to look down the street. "It was lovely down by the shore, but it is very good to be back. Nothing like home, you know?"

Bev turned to admire the inn. "You said it."

~

Bev worked diligently, and before she knew it, all the windows of the Weary Dragon were gleaming in the early afternoon sun. She tossed the dirty rag into the pail and admired her handiwork for a moment. The inn was two stories, with a thatched roof and white walls. The front door was new, thanks to the sinkhole fiasco, as were the empty flower boxes out front. It was still a bit too early for those, but not for the other gardening task she'd planned for the day.

Her herb garden was around back, next to the stable where Sin (short for Sinister), her trusty mule, was housed. The old girl had spent most of the winter in there, save a few trips to the flour mill when the roads were passable, but today, she was out in her pen, enjoying the early spring sun. Bev nodded to her as she dragged an almost-outgrowing-the-pot rosemary bush from inside the kitchen.

She placed the rosemary to the side and dug her fingers into the black, cool soil. Familiarity swelled in her chest as she inhaled the scent of crumbling earth. A small, light brown nose poked out from under her arm and started sniffing, too.

"Don't you even think about digging up this garden, Mr. Biscuit," Bev warned her laelaps. "You'd better guard this rosemary plant with your life, understand?"

The dog opened his mouth, unfurling his pink tongue, which Bev usually took to mean "yes."

She pulled the rosemary out of its pot, tapping the root bed to loosen the dirt and roots then settled it in the hole she'd dug, right where it had been before. Rosemary was hardy and could survive even the harshest Pigsend winter. But during the Harvest Festival, a disguised queen's soldier had set his own magic-detection creature to the garden, destroying it almost completely in the overzealous search for magic.

Magic. Bev had done a good job of forgetting about that word, what with all the strange visions she got when she thought too much about it. It had started with finding a piece of an amulet right here in the garden—one the soldier's magic detector hadn't noticed. Then she'd found another piece, and when she put them together, she'd gotten a terrible vision about a bloody battle, perhaps during the war five years ago. More pieces had fallen into place when, in a conversation with Vellora Witzel, Bev had realized which one—a particularly infamous one full of atrocities on both sides.

Now, all that was a bit much for a simple innkeeper, so Bev just buried it deep in her mind, just like she was burying the rosemary. Once she'd finished that, she turned to the hardier of her herbs that had also been growing in the window—thyme, oregano, and chives. The basil would remain indoors while she waited for warmer weather, as would the parsley.

A loud call echoed through the open kitchen door, catching Bev's attention. It was still a bit early for travelers, but not unheard of. Bev stood, washed her hands under the water pump, and headed toward the front room, Biscuit trotting at her feet.

The bottom floor of the Weary Dragon consisted of two main spaces—the kitchen, where Bev did her work, and the front room, which doubled as a welcome area and dining room in the evening. And it was there Bev found three old women. Having already taken off their traveling cloaks, they were wearing patched and mended dresses that splayed out from their generous hips and tops. One had gray, almost bluish hair. Another, shorter, had red hair with white stripes. And the shortest had light gray hair. They seemed to share some features, though the redhead and the blue-haired shared the most.

"Good afternoon," Bev said, approaching the counter and taking her well-worn guest book from the shelf below. "Welcome to the Weary Dragon. You'll be staying the night?"

"Oh, yes," the tallest of the group said. "My name is Janet Hester." She pointed to the redhead. "This is my sister, Rita." She pointed to the shortest. "And our cousin, Gladys Hester."

"Glad to have you," Bev said. "Will you be needing two or three rooms?" She glanced at their poorly mended clothes, wondering if they wanted to hear the price before she wrote their names down. "It's one gold piece per room per night, if that suits you. It does include dinner."

"Just three beds," Janet said with a jovial smile as she placed two gold coins on the counter.

"Two rooms, then," Bev said, scribbling their names in her visitor's log and retrieving the keys. "Rooms one and two. Make it simple." Bev glanced around for any luggage but they carried very little. Just a small handbag apiece. Not unheard of, but quite unusual. "Please make yourselves at home, and let me know if you need anything," Bev said. "I'll be in the kitchen."

"Very kind," Rita said. "You've got a lovely place here."

"And a lovely village," Gladys added.

"Is this your first time in Pigsend?" Bev asked, and they nodded. "What brings you to town?"

"Oh, this and that," Janet replied, gazing at the ceiling.

Beasts and Baking

"Just passing through." Rita smoothed her clothes.

Gladys tilted her head with a wide smile. "Traveling the country, you know."

Clearly, they wanted to keep their business private. "Well, if you're staying a while, we have a lovely tea shop in town, and a nice library. I'll let the baker next door know we've got guests so he'll drop off some pastries."

"Oh, how lovely!" Gladys clapped and grinned.

Janet nodded fervently. "Just the thing."

"I do love—*Oh, my!*" Rita jumped, revealing Mr. Biscuit on his hind legs behind her, sniffing the air. "What in the world is this? A dog?"

"*Biscuit*," Bev scolded, hurrying around the front of the desk to shoo him away. "So sorry about that. He's a bit too curious for his own good."

But all three ladies melted into looks of complete adoration as they knelt and held out their hands for him to sniff. Biscuit obliged, watching them warily before deciding they were nice enough and wagging his tail.

"What a love," Rita said, scratching the sweet spot right at the base of his tail.

Janet had found his velvety ears. "Such a sweet thing,"

"I do love dogs," Gladys said, reaching under to rub his belly.

Biscuit collapsed to the ground, rolling onto his

back and exposing his belly. His tongue fell out of his mouth as he enjoyed what were *clearly* the best belly rubs he'd ever had.

"You'd better cut that out or you'll never be rid of him," Bev said with a knowing smile. "But in all seriousness, he's something of a food thief, so make sure to watch your dinner bowls this evening." She snapped her fingers. "Which reminds me, I should pop over to the butcher to double my order."

"Better make it a triple," Janet said, slowly rising.

Rita reached into her pocket and slid over another gold coin. "We do enjoy eating."

Bev smiled, pushing the coin back. She wasn't about to order nine pounds of meat for seven people. But the ladies didn't need to know that. "Will do."

They bustled up the stairs, complimenting everything from the paneling to the stair railing to the floors Bev hadn't yet waxed. They were either the nicest guests Bev had ever hosted or there was something amiss about them.

Biscuit whined as he rolled onto his back, watching them go. Being a laelaps, Biscuit usually only reacted when there was food…or a magical object or person nearby. The old ladies seemed normal enough, but one never knew what could be hidden beneath the surface.

"They didn't have any dried beef up their

sleeves, did they?" Bev asked, almost under her breath.

The laelaps turned his head up at her inquisitively.

"Let's just leave them be," she said with a shake of her head. "You know, it's a new season, and I'm sure they won't be the last magical folk to pass through town. Might as well get into the habit of leaving them alone." She paused, giving him an intent look. "You hear? Leave them be, Mr. Biscuit."

He turned and trotted back toward the kitchen.

"Good boy," Bev said with a satisfied sigh.

The Weary Dragon Inn was officially back in business for another year.

Chapter Two

"What a spread!"

Rita, Janet, and Gladys stood ready with plates in their hands as Bev brought out the platter of sausages resting on a bed of potato and parsnip mash. The ladies eyed the meat, almost greedily, and Bev barely got the platter on the table before they dug in.

"Is this…all the food we'll be having this evening?" Janet asked, pausing as the spoon hovered over the platter.

"I've got two loaves of rosemary bread in there, too," Bev said. "Should be plenty for seven."

"*Seven*?" Gladys frowned, sharing a disappointed look with Rita.

"Well, all right," the other woman said heavily. "We'll wait until the rest show up before we come back for seconds."

Bev was a little taken aback as she returned to the kitchen to retrieve the bread. She'd gotten a little over five pounds of meat from the butcher, which amounted to nearly three quarters of a pound per person. More than Bev could eat, for sure, and the three regulars were usually around half a pound each.

Speaking of the regulars, by the time Bev returned to the front room, they were already helping themselves, looking overjoyed at the change of pace.

"Meat!" Etheldra Daws was the old, taciturn owner of the only tea shop in town. Today, though, she looked on the verge of shedding joyful tears as she scooped sausage onto her plate. "Finally. Not sure I could've stomached another night of that *dreadful* barley soup."

Bev swallowed her response. "Yes, the butchers are back in town."

"Did Ida and Vellora have a good trip?" Bardoff Boyd was the young local schoolmaster. He was short and eager, with bright eyes and a perpetual optimistic grin. "They were gone a while."

"They did. Ida was glowing," Bev said. "Even Vellora seemed to be in much better spirits."

"Yes, well, they should think hard about leaving

us all in the lurch," Etheldra said, sitting down at one of the three round tables. "This town gets by on meat. If the butchers are gone, who'll be around to feed us?"

"They were only gone a fortnight," Bev said with a roll of her eyes.

Earl was the third of the trio of regulars to get his plate. "How did window washing go today?"

"Got it all done," Bev said. "I'll bring the ladder by in the morning."

"Nonsense." He waved her off. "Where is it? I'll grab it and bring it back when I head home."

"Round the back," Bev said. "If you're sure—"

He was, he insisted, so Bev relented. He joined his fellow diners at the second round table in the room. The regulars didn't seem interested in chatting up Bev's guests, but the guests themselves seemed a little preoccupied with a small brown nose and white paws that had popped up on their table.

"Biscuit," Bev chided. "Feel free to tell him to leave you alone."

"Oh, he's just a doll," Rita said, standing with her empty bowl. Bev was a bit surprised; hadn't they just sat? "May we have seconds? That is, of course, assuming we're not expecting more folks this evening?"

"This should do it," Bev said.

Rita turned, counting the heads. "Surely, you have more guests than just us."

Beasts and Baking

"It's still early in the season," Bev explained. "Not many folks ready to brave the cold and mud just yet. But give it a few weeks, and this place'll be bustling." She nodded to the trio of usuals. "Etheldra, Bardoff, and Earl are from here, of course, and come to dinner nearly every night. Sometimes Max Sterling, the librarian, joins us. But I think he's off visiting his nephew in Middleburg."

"I see." Rita glanced around the room. "If you're sure it's all right to have more."

"Help yourself," Bev said. "The more you eat, the less I have to clean."

The other two ladies helped themselves as well, and Gladys even came around for thirds with a meek look. By the time the ladies were through, there was nary a crumb left on any of the plates.

"You sure do eat," Etheldra said with a side eye to the sisters. "Where do you put it?"

"Etheldra, don't be rude," Bardoff snapped. "I can't blame them for wanting more."

Etheldra snorted, as if wanting to disagree. "Where are you three coming from? Bit cold to travel, don't you think? Must be important business. Not much going on in town these days."

Bev could hardly believe it, but all three beamed at her as if she were the most adorable curiosity they'd ever seen.

"Enough to be getting on with!" Janet said.

"You'd be surprised at the kinds of things that

go on in a small town."

"It's also just nice to sit and knit for a change."

"Well, are you here for business or to knit?" Etheldra asked, her gaze narrowing.

"I think their business is their own," Bev replied with a thin smile. She'd have to disinvite the tea shop owner until these women moved on if Etheldra was going to be so inquisitive. There was nothing to be curious about—nothing had happened in town to arouse suspicion.

"Too right you are, Bev!" Rita replied with a bright smile. "Did I hear you own the tea shop? That's quite a lovely business!"

"We should visit in the morning," Janet said.

"I hear you'll have sweets," Gladys said.

"Aye. But you didn't answer my question—"

"Etheldra, whatever business they have in town is theirs." Bev smiled at Etheldra, silently hoping the other woman would get the hint and stop harassing her guests.

"Harrumph." Message received. "I've got half a mind to head over to the butchers this evening. Sausage is only moderately acceptable. I do expect beef or chicken tomorrow. Their vacation is over, and there are *clearly* hungry mouths to feed in town." She glanced at the three old women. "Will you be staying another night?"

Janet beamed. "Perhaps."

"We'll definitely be to your shop in the

morning," Rita said.

"I do love a good sweet," Gladys said.

"Harrumph." The three women's sunny demeanor didn't seem to permeate Etheldra's usual brusqueness. "I suppose I'll see you tomorrow, Bev."

Bev nodded. "Have a good night, Etheldra."

"I'll just grab that ladder," Earl said, donning his hat. "Have a good evening, Bev. Ladies." He tipped his cap to them and followed Etheldra out the door.

"Early night for you, too, Bardoff?" Bev asked the schoolteacher.

"As always," he said with a chuckle. "But I did want to ask if we were still on for tomorrow?"

Bev stared at him, her mind drawing a blank. "Tomorrow? What's tomorrow?"

"Yes, um…" He glanced at the three ladies, who were back at the serving platter, searching for any more morsels of food. "I'm bringing the children by for a lesson."

Bev slapped her forehead. "Of course! So sorry. Completely slipped my mind. Yes, please. Be happy to, uh…" She chuckled nervously. "What am I teaching them, exactly? And why?"

"I was hoping you'd give us some insight into the life of an innkeeper. Perhaps give us a look inside the day-to-day, how you manage to keep this place running."

"Oh, well… I just do what Wim taught me," Bev said, feeling a bit out of place. "Why is that something the kids need to know?"

"It's important for the children to get exposed to different industries," he said. "Many of them come from the farmlands, and most don't know a life outside Pigsend. But given some exposure, some might decide to pursue a different path." He patted his chest. "I sure did."

"Oh?" Bev didn't know much about the schoolteacher's background. "Are you from here?"

"Well, not here exactly, but close enough," he said. "The old schoolmaster opened my mind to a world outside shepherding, and I left Pigsend to attend school in Queen's Capital. Returned here and took over when he retired."

"I see." Bev could've argued he didn't make it far out of Pigsend, even if he'd opted to become a teacher instead of a farmer. "Well, I'll do my best, but I'm not quite sure I'll be the best teacher. Most of my day is pretty boring."

"Nonsense. The children are eager to learn how you make your famous bread," Bardoff said.

"Oh, uh…" Bev rubbed the back of her head. "I do try to keep that something of a secret, you know. Planning on entering the Harvest Festival and—"

"You don't have to tell us specifics, of course," he said with a wave of his hand. "I was hoping to use the breadmaking as a science lesson."

"Science?" Bev frowned. "What do you mean?"

"Well, the temperature you bake the bread, the

rise of the dough, the amounts you use of flour and water and rosemary…" He lifted a shoulder. "Surely, you'll be able to tell the children how all that goes together."

"Only that it does," Bev said, regretting the decision to volunteer. "Like I said. I just do what ol' Wim McKee taught me. Don't really measure much. Don't even keep a temperature gauge in the kitchen. It's all done by feel."

The teacher wasn't deterred. "Well, I'm sure you'll impart some nuggets of wisdom anyway. The kids got some good insights from Rustin, even, so I'm sure you'll do great. From what I learned in college, baking is quite scientific."

"More like magic, in my estimation," Gladys chimed in from one of the chairs by the fire. She'd pulled a large ball of yarn from her threadbare bag and settled down.

"No, not magic," Bev said, though she had to brush off the uncomfortable feeling that rose in her chest. "Just knowledge passed down from one innkeeper to another. Not much that'll educate a bunch of school kids."

"I'm sure you have plenty to offer them," Bardoff said, slipping his cloak on. "I'll see you in the morning, Bev."

She gave him a half-hearted goodbye as he slipped out the door into the cold night, and she put her hands on her hips, shaking her head.

"Can't be easy for a schoolmaster in a farm town," Rita said, sitting down in the chair across from Gladys. "I'm sure most of the kids will end up farming like their parents."

"Oh, come now, Rita," Janet said, loudly scraping a chair across the room and settling down in it. She pulled a ball of thin yarn from her bag, too —this one multicolored. "There's plenty to teach. Reading, mathematics, how to read a calendar, history—"

"History!" Gladys scoffed. "Don't be teaching that too loudly, or the queen'll send her minions after you."

The trio twittered as they pulled out various knitting needles and crochet hooks, along with their projects. Gladys's looked to be a crocheted shawl, Rita's was a pair of mittens, and Janet was working on matching socks. Each was made from different scraps of yarn to form a multicolored object, and Bev was starting to get the impression their patchwork of clothes wasn't because they were poor; rather, they seemed to like the style.

"Did you fight in the war, Bev?" Rita asked.

Bev went rigid.

The stench of blood, the feeling of magic zipping through her veins, and the simultaneous thrill and dread of impending battle swam in her mind. The wall of people…

"No," Bev said with a firm smile. "Well, if I did,

I can't remember. No clue who I was before I showed up in town five years ago."

That was her story, and she was sticking to it, no matter what sort of memories threatened to resurface about battles and wars and iron bangles and fighting for the kingside alongside Vellora. The butcher had never said a word about recognizing Bev, so perhaps…perhaps these visions were just the result of an overactive imagination. Either way, the past was in the past, and Bev was quite content to spend her days washing windows and baking bread.

The ladies seemed to buy it and began talking amongst themselves as they worked the yarn.

"Are you three set for the evening?" Bev asked, clearing her throat. "Anything else I can do?"

"Oh, we'll just sit here by the fire all night and knit," Gladys said with a kind smile. "Everything was lovely."

"The baker should be bringing muffins by in the morning," Bev said. "What time will you be leaving?"

Rita stopped, glancing at her sister. "Oh, well. We're not quite sure if we're moving on yet. Depends on what tomorrow brings."

"Hopefully, not snow," Bev said with a grimace. She'd had her fill of that—and the guests who'd been stuck here—during the solstice.

"No, not snow," Janet replied with a chuckle. "We've got some business in town we'll need to resolve before we move on."

"Good to know," Bev said with a nod. "Please, stay as long as you need, then."

~

Bev awoke the next morning and groaned as she remembered Bardoff would be bringing the children by. She really didn't have much experience teaching, but she had to humor one of her best customers. And she did understand what Bardoff was trying to do, even if she didn't consider herself the right woman for the job.

The inn was cold, so Bev started the fires in the kitchen and front room to be ready for the three ladies to come down. Bev had begun calling them "grannies" in her mind, because they seemed the sort to dote on a bevy of grandchildren. They were odd but seemed harmless enough. And Bev was certainly glad for the two gold coins they'd paid.

She set to her morning chores—feeding Biscuit and Sin—along with scrubbing any final pots and pans from last night's meal, getting her bread dough on its first rise of the day. She'd used the last of her hanging rosemary, so she set out to the garden to check on her transplanted plant—

And found it almost a foot taller than it had been the day before.

"Guess you really like being back in the garden," Bev muttered, snipping off a few branches.

Or is it the magic in the soil? that nasty little voice

asked.

"Hush now." But she couldn't help but notice Biscuit was interested in the clippings. "And you, cut it out. Nothing interesting about my rosemary except the flavor."

Bev had just finished hanging the rosemary sprigs in the window to dry when Allen Mackey walked in the front door with a basket of muffins. He was a young fellow, tall with dark hair, and seemed happy this morning.

"Morning, Bev," he called. "Feels nice and warm in here."

"Morning, Allen," she said, wiping her hands on her apron. "What do you have for me today?"

"Orange cranberry," he said.

"Oh, how exotic," Bev said, inhaling the scent of the muffins. "Where'd you get the oranges?"

"Ida and Vellora brought me back some from their trip," he said. "Etheldra *has* been asking for some new options lately, so I thought these might do the trick." He put the basket on the counter. "How many guests did you say you had last night?"

"Three," Bev said, taking three off the top and putting them on the table. "I'm sure they'll be down soon."

"Take one for yourself, too." Allen handed her one off the top. "I'm dying to know what you think."

Bev picked up one of the muffins, inhaling the

scent. "They smell heavenly." She took a bite. "And taste heavenly, too."

"Oh, is that breakfast?"

The grannies appeared at the top of the stairs, hurrying down faster than Bev would've thought possible at their age. They snatched all the muffins in the basket and devoured them within seconds—then went for the three on the table, too.

"Absolutely fantastic," Rita said, licking her fingers.

Janet beamed at Allen. "You're quite an adept baker, young man."

"Is there more?" Gladys peered inside the basket.

"There will be more at Etheldra's tea shop," Allen said with a look to Bev. "After, *ahem*, I bake them…"

"Etheldra?" Gladys brightened. "Oh, she was quite a dear, wasn't she?"

"Just the sweetest." Rita nodded.

Janet joined in. "Thought she was just a *delight*."

Bev and Allen shared a confused look. "Etheldra? A dear?" Allen said, rubbing the back of his head. "That's a new one."

With their bellies full, the grannies returned to the chairs and pulled out their knitting projects, talking amongst themselves as they'd done the night before.

"Well, I suppose I'd better get back to the shop," Allen said, looking at his empty basket a little forlornly. "Etheldra'll be mad if I don't have the muffins there when she opens. But I suppose it's time to start baking more, what with things warming up for the spring. Good thing the Witzels brought me a crate of oranges."

He bade her farewell and disappeared through the front door.

"He seems like a nice young man," Janet said.

"He's quite lovely," Bev said, before glancing at the clock. "Goodness me, I've got to get in the kitchen and get things sorted before those children arrive."

"Oh, that's right!" Rita smiled. "We may stick around and listen, if that's all right."

"I'm... Well, I'm not sure it'll be that interesting," Bev said. "But you're welcome to stay."

Chapter Three

At exactly nine-thirty, the front door opened and seventeen schoolchildren filed into the kitchen, followed by an excited Bardoff. Bev had seen the kids around town and knew some of them by their parents, but the schoolteacher asked each kid to introduce themselves. With only one teacher in town, they ranged in ages from tiny Tallulah Punter, who had recently turned six, to Vicky's brother Grant Hamblin, who was nearly fourteen.

"And this is Bev," Bardoff said after the group was finished. "Just Bev, right?"

"Just Bev," she replied with a nod. She didn't want to explain it was short for "Beverage Wench" because that was the job Wim McKee had given her when she'd showed up in town.

"Indeed." Bardoff took a seat. "Well, Bev. You have the floor!"

At once, seventeen pairs of young eyes faced her.

"So…" She cleared her throat. "What have you guys learned about baking so far?"

There was a chorus of mumbling Bardoff was kind enough to translate. "They know the basics. Add heat to cook things, but not the why. Thought I'd give you the honors."

"Well," Bev coughed nervously, "to be honest, I'm not sure why either."

Bardoff sprung upright, a movement he seemed quite practiced at, and addressed the students. "Students, we cook things to change their composition, right? Nobody wants to eat raw dough. Different levels of heat provide different results. Turn it too high for too long, and you end up with ash. Too low and too short, it'll be undercooked. There's an artistry to getting the temperature just right, isn't there, Bev?"

Bev had to agree. Wim had taught her the precise temperature at which to bake bread by feel alone. "And it depends on the weather, too."

"The weather?" Bardoff's smile grew as if he knew the answer to the question he was asking. "How so?"

"Well, take the rosemary bread, for example," Bev said. "If it's dreary outside, I need to add more flour or more firewood. If it's cold, too, same thing. You just sort of have to…well, know what you're doing to remember it all."

"Fascinating," Bardoff said. "So you make bread every day?"

"Mostly, though I tend to slack off in the late summer months when it gets quite hot," Bev said.

"And how do you make your famous bread?" Bardoff asked. When Bev hedged, he added, "No need to divulge any secrets, of course. Just the basics."

"I start with a bit of flour, my starter, some salt, and rosemary from my garden," Bev said. "Water, too. Some barm from the beer I brew."

"And what is starter?" Bardoff asked.

"Usually, it's a bit of bread from the day before," she said. "Helps get things going. You mix all that together, knead it for a bit, then let it proof for a few hours—depends on the weather and temperature, of course—then you'll want to shape it and get it into loaf pans for another rise. Then, about an hour or two before dinner, I'll stick it in the oven to bake. Let it cool for another hour, then it's time to cut into it." She held up one finger. "If there's one thing Wim McKee was clear about, you *never* cut into bread until it's completely cooled. You want it to finish cooking out of the oven. Can't do that if you let all the steam escape."

She paused, gauging the interest from the

children. Grant Hamblin was whispering with two others—Valta Climber, the younger sister of the blacksmith's apprentice Gilda, and PJ Norris, the son of two farriers.

"Bev, would it be all right if the children helped you bake bread for this evening?" Bardoff asked.

"Well, I've already got this evening's batch proofing," Bev said, gesturing to her proofing baskets near the fire. "But maybe we could use a little bit of the starter and barm and make some more?"

Bev didn't have enough starter to give each kid their own ball of dough, so they had to split into groups of three or four. She meted out flour, water, starter, and salt (leaving out the rosemary), and instructed the kids to blend it then how to knead the bread.

Unfortunately, there wasn't much to instruct—as much as Bardoff kept asking "how much" or "what temperature," Bev was woefully lacking in her specifics. When it came to her famous rosemary bread, the dough came together by touch rather than by any measurement.

"See, it depends," Bev said a little tersely, when Bardoff prompted her again. "Ol' Wim McKee used to come by and touch the dough when I'd make it until I knew exactly how it was supposed to feel."

She walked over to Valta and touched the dough she was working on with Grant and PJ. "More water. See how it's a little too tacky?"

The girl glanced at her two friends, shrugging.

"It feels sticky to me?" PJ said, poking his hand in the dough.

Bev added a little more water and instructed Valta to knead it again. "See the difference?"

"No."

"Well…" Bev put her hand on her hip. "Well, there's a difference."

"If you say so."

Bardoff wasn't deterred. "Why do you think we have to knead the bread, children?"

A few shrugs, a couple of bored sighs, and one small giggle came from the group.

"Bev, what happens if you don't knead the bread enough?" Bardoff asked.

"Uh… Well, to tell you the truth, I never deviated from what Wim told me, so I'm—"

Bardoff sighed. "The bread doesn't rise correctly! You'll get a flat bread that tastes all right, but isn't quite what you want. Bev, how long do you usually knead your bread?"

Bev did actually know that answer. "Ten minutes, give or take. It's really more based on feel than time."

"And what do you do after you finish kneading it?" Bardoff asked.

"Put it in a warm spot to proof," Bev said. "That takes a few hours, depending on the temperature—

and *no,* Bardoff, I don't know what temperature it is. You just kind of know what's too warm and too cold after you do it for a few years."

"Perhaps we could try an experiment," Bardoff said. "Could we put our bread in the oven now and see what happens?"

Bev rubbed the back of her neck. "I'm not sure that's a good idea," she said. "I don't want to mess with the oven. I'm using it to proof tonight's bread, and you don't want to see Etheldra if there isn't any rosemary bread."

"Well, perhaps the children can take their dough home and try it there," Bardoff said with a thin smile. "Children, why don't you get back to kneading your dough, and we can talk about how the texture changes. Bev, you can…um…tend to the night's bread."

There wasn't much to tend to yet, but she did show the children what it looked like mid-proof and the difference between that and the dough they were working on. They seemed about as interested as PJ, Valta, and Grant, who weren't as much kneading their dough as smearing it into the table (*That'll be fun to clean up*, Bev thought with a grimace). The only one who looked to be having fun was tiny Tallulah, who was squealing in delight as she squeezed the dough between her fingers.

Bev crossed the room to speak with Bardoff, who seemed oblivious to the discontent in his ranks.

"Bardoff," she said in a low voice. "I'm not quite sure they're getting much out of this…er…lesson."

"Nonsense," he said with a satisfied smile. "They're learning about bread."

Bev glanced at where Valta and PJ were throwing pieces of dough at each other. "Are they, though?"

"It might not seem like it," he said. "But hands-on experience is so important."

Grant had joined in, tossing little pellets of dough at his two friends.

"Did you learn that at Queen's Capital?" Bev asked. "All about baking and rise and dough formation?"

"Oh, yes. We had all manner of classes at the university," he said. "Lots of instruction on how to teach, but also learning ourselves. Several sessions on the sciences—the queen is very interested in science and engineering."

Just not magic, Bev thought idly.

"We also studied math and history." He paused. "Well, some history. The war's effects hit the scholars like everyone else."

Bev didn't know enough to ask what he meant by that. "It sounds like you really enjoyed your time there."

He nodded. "It really was a transformative experience for a farm kid like me. I'd love it if even *one* of my students gets to see the world outside their farms."

"Well, Valta's sister's a blacksmith's apprentice," Bev said, pointing at the girl who was laughing as she tried to smear dough over her friend's face. "That's a bit off the farm, isn't it?"

"Bev, you need to think *bigger!* Surely, you know…" He paused, perhaps remembering Bev had no memory of the world outside Pigsend. "Well, maybe *you* don't know, but there's so much to explore and see and do. These kids need to understand they can be anything they want to be."

"And what if what they want to be is a simple farmer?"

Bardoff sighed, and some of his optimistic facade fell away. "Most of them will be, to be honest. It's a miracle if I can get them to come to class—most of them disappear in the spring when the planting starts and again in the fall during the harvest. The winter months are the only time I can get their undivided attention. So I try to expose them to as many options as possible under the guise of *learning* and hope maybe one of them is inspired, as I was."

"I'm afraid I'm not doing much inspiring," Bev said. "Most of them could learn to bake at their parents' houses. And 'innkeeper' isn't a job that's in high demand."

"Well, perhaps learning about some of the science will inspire them to—" Bardoff's face changed. "Knock it off."

She turned. Valta, PJ, and Grant's dough pellet throwing had turned into tossing large wads at each other—and getting flour involved, too. But Bardoff's admonition was ignored by the trio, and the other kids joined in.

"Stop!" Bardoff called, running to the center. "Stop it this instant!"

Bev watched helplessly as the kitchen disappeared in a plume of flour, punctuated by the sound of children's laughter. Biscuit, aroused from his slumber by the excitement, began barking and running around, gathering white dust on his golden fur.

"Stop! Children, stop! You're not being very good guests!" Bardoff was rushing around in the chaos, but he didn't seem to be doing much to stop the frenzied throwing of flour.

Finally, Bev put her fingers to her mouth and whistled loudly. Immediately, the laughter stopped, though the flour took longer to settle. When it did, a light sheen of dust covered every inch of the kitchen, from the herb tins on the top shelf to the stone floor.

"*Children*," Bardoff said through gritted teeth. Bev had never seen the schoolmaster look so angry. He seemed unable to form words as he pointed to the wall by the door. The children followed his unspoken command and queued up single-file against the wall, their heads hanging in shame. Bardoff walked along the line and plucked the three instigators from it, marching them to stand in front of Bev.

"*Apologize*," he said, his grip firm on Valta and PJ's shoulders, Grant squeezed in between them. "*Now*."

"Sorry, Bev," the trio muttered.

"It's gonna take me a bit to clean this up," Bev said. "Probably could use some help."

"Good idea," Bardoff said, walking to face the three with murder on his face. "You will clean this kitchen until Bev says it's okay to leave. I don't care if it takes all day and night."

"But—" PJ began, earning a silencing glare from Bardoff.

"You know," Bev said, after a long pause, "I find the *best* lessons come from the natural consequences of our actions. So, perhaps it was a good idea for the kids to be here today." She gave Bardoff a kind smile. "I'll see you at dinner tonight?"

―

Bev wasn't sure how much she'd have to keep on the kids, but she was actually impressed with their work ethic. All three set to scrubbing every inch of the kitchen, leaving no pot or shelf untouched. To their credit, they kept their heads down and didn't speak a word to each other, or to Bev. Even Biscuit seemed to keep his distance, watching them work with his curious golden eyes.

When the clock struck five, Bev decided to let them off the hook. There were still a few spots of flour, but nothing she couldn't tackle during the deep clean she still had to do.

"That's fine for this evening," Bev said, turning to them with her hands on her hips. "Hope you three learned your lesson about wasting good flour."

Grant elbowed his compatriots. "Um... We're really sorry we made a mess in here, Bev."

Valta nodded. "Sorry, Bev."

"Sorry," PJ mumbled after Valta elbowed him.

Bev nodded to the basket of warm rosemary bread she'd just pulled from the oven. "Now get on home. And no more cutting up during Bardoff's lessons, do you understand?"

They snatched a slice each and tumbled through the kitchen door. Bev watched them with a little smile on her face. Kids would be kids, after all.

Bev spent the next hour finalizing dinner while the rest of the rosemary bread cooled. Etheldra would be pleased with the beef roast and carrots, and there would be *plenty* for even the hearty appetites of the grannies, who'd already come down and were waiting patiently in the dining room.

At five past six, Bardoff, Etheldra, and Earl arrived, and Etheldra let out a harrumph of appreciation when she scented the night's meal. Bardoff split from them and walked over to Bev, weariness on his face.

"I hope that Grant, PJ, and Valta did a good job," he said.

Bev nodded. "They did. They're good kids. Just got a bit too excited."

"I agree. They're my three brightest students. I'd hate for them to go down the wrong path."

"Go eat and take a load off," Bev said with a nod. "All's well that ends well."

He nodded gratefully and plated his food. As soon as he was gone, the grannies swarmed and filled their plates with the rest of the food. Bev couldn't believe the quantities they packed in—especially as she'd asked Ida to send over more than the usual amount. But they'd paid another two gold coins for their rooms, so she really couldn't—

A loud rumbling filled the room, turning every head.

"What in the...?" Earl said, looking up.

Bev braced herself for the ground to start shaking, but even when it didn't, she didn't feel any better.

"Do you think it's another sinkhole?" Bardoff asked.

"It was definitely something," Etheldra said, casting her suspicious gaze at the three grannies.

"Certainly loud enough." None of the grannies looked pleased. "Perhaps we should go check on it."

All seven of those in the inn walked outside. Bev

expected to see a gaping hole in front of the inn—but there wasn't. A gust of wind blew by, bringing with it the scent of burning timber. A red tint edged the sky, and the group turned north at the sound of shrieking. Bev's heart went out to Earl as the old carpenter led the group, his face growing more and more concerned as they drew closer to his part of town, his street, his house…

His workshop was up in flames.

Chapter Four

The fire was so large and sudden, it drew a crowd immediately. But the good people of Pigsend weren't the sort to sit back and let a building burn down. Anyone who was close grabbed a bucket, and they all formed a line to nearby Pigsend Creek. Bev joined the line, standing between Pip Norris and his wife Holly as she moved empty buckets one way and took full buckets the other.

But even as fast as everyone moved, the fire was too much for poor Earl's workshop, and before too long, it was nothing but a heap of burning ash.

"Oh, Earl," Bev said, putting her hand on his shoulder as he stoically stared at the embers. "I'm so sorry."

He wiped his face with his handkerchief, perhaps a few tears mixed with the sweat on his face. "It'll be fine. I can rebuild. That's what I do, you know? Fix things that are broken." He sniffed and rubbed his nose.

Bev was at a loss for how to comfort him. Earl had sprung into action when the front of Bev's inn had fallen into the sinkhole, and he'd rebuilt the Brewer twins' house, too. He was the go-to man in the town when something broke, and it just didn't seem fair he'd have to repair his own workshop.

"Just hate I lost all those chairs. Hendry's gonna be furious." He let out a watery chuckle.

"Hendry had better hold her tongue, or else," Ida said, coming to stand beside him. "Can't blame you for a freak fire in your workshop."

"Suppose not," he said, kicking a nearby black piece of wood. "Oh, what a mess."

Ida caught Bev's expression and nodded. "Don't you worry, Earl. We're going to help you clean all this up. And rebuild!"

"We are?" Vellora said. "Ida, you don't know the first thing about building—"

"I can carry wood, can't I?" Ida huffed. "Earl's been the backbone of this town for decades. It's the least we can do."

"Agreed." Bev nodded firmly.

"We're in, too." Shasta and Stella, the twins whose house was destroyed during the sinkhole fiasco, put down the half-empty bucket they'd been carrying and stood next to Ida. "Whatever you need, Earl."

"And me," Allen said.

"As much as I appreciate it," Earl said with a wet laugh, "I don't think any of you know how to swing a hammer or measure or cut or—"

"Then you can tell us what to do," Bev said. "Or maybe we'll just provide pastries and tea and muscle."

"I'm sure Etheldra will have to approve that," Earl said to Shasta, who worked at the tea shop.

"Approved." The old woman patted her dear friend on the shoulder before surveying the damage with a curious look. "Now what in the world happened here?"

"Clearly, a fire." Mayor Jo Hendry appeared out of the darkness, conveniently after all the work was done. She tutted sadly and took Earl's hands in hers. "My dear Earl, I'm devastated to hear about your workshop. So many beautiful items."

"Your chairs," he said. "I'm sorry."

"Well." She forced a smile, but there was tension behind it. "That's on me for not picking them up earlier. I suppose you'll just have to make them again."

"I think he'll probably focus on rebuilding his workshop first," Bev said.

"Of course, of course." She bristled. "But that'll

take a day, right?"

"I don't—"

"I'll be in touch, Earl. Keep your chin up!" Hendry called, disappearing back into the darkness.

"I think the next election, someone *else* should run for her office," Vellora said.

"Good luck with that," Bev said. She had a sinking suspicion that if someone did want to run against Hendry, the beloved mayor might cast a spell to convince them it was a bad idea. Hendry seemed to have an uncanny ability to control a room—and people—though Bev wasn't quite sure what kind of magic she possessed.

"Suppose I should prioritize her chairs, hm?" Earl said. "She has been waiting."

"She can wait longer," Ida snapped. "You can't make chairs without a workshop. And all your tools…" She kicked a nearby ember. "I do hope we can find them in all this."

"Probably have to wait until the morning when it all cools off," Earl said. "Can't believe it burned down so quickly."

"Yes. It's strange," Etheldra said, turning to look at Bev.

"What is?"

"This fire." She slowly knelt near the embers. "Earl's careful with his flammables, aren't you, Earl?"

"Of course, but you know, accidents happen.

Who's to say it was something in the shop?" Earl said. "Maybe a passing ember from a chimney or—"

"Or someone set the fire," Etheldra said, her gaze practically boring a hole into Bev.

"Oh, come now." Bev laughed, a little nervously. "Why are you looking at me? There's a sheriff in town who—"

"Rustin?" Ida scoffed. "He can barely investigate his way to his office each morning."

"Besides that, *you're* the resident mystery solver," Etheldra replied plainly. "And this is very clearly a mystery."

Bev opened her mouth to argue, but everyone in the group was looking the same way. She put her hands on her hips and scowled. "I'm *not* the resident mystery solver. I'm just… Things just happen to…" She couldn't quite form the words to argue. "Besides that, this isn't a mystery. It's *one* fire. If the whole town goes up in flames, I'll be sure to break out my glowing stick and investigate."

Earl's mournful sigh softened her stance. "I know it's not your thing, Bev, but it would mean a lot if you could… Maybe it'll help me sleep better at night knowin' it was just an accident, and not someone…"

"Oh, all right," Bev said. "Why don't I come by tomorrow morning?"

~

Bev went to bed convinced she was going to talk

with Earl about hypotheticals and walk away with him understanding that accidents happen. But as she lay awake with Biscuit snoring between her calves, she couldn't help but remember something *odd* about how he'd asked to speak with her privately. Something unreadable in the old man's face.

And perhaps he wanted to speak with her in private not because he was tired, but because he had information he didn't want shared with the wider group.

Either way, Bev rose and did her chores, setting aside a second tea mug and putting on the kettle. She kept an ear out for the grannies upstairs and for Earl or Allen at the front door while Biscuit watched her with wary golden eyes.

"Not sleeping this morning?" Bev asked the laelaps while she worked her rosemary bread dough. "Is something magical afoot?"

He let out a low sniff.

"Hm." Bev slowed her kneading. "Well, let's see what Earl has to say."

At a quarter past seven, Allen arrived with cream-filled pastries dusted with candied orange peel, and, like the day before, the moment he walked into the inn, the upstairs floorboards started creaking.

"Hope you didn't bring the whole batch this time," Bev said with a chuckle.

Beasts and Baking

"Made double this morning and left half back in the bakery." He winked. "But I will say, the ladies were so nice yesterday. Came by mid-afternoon just as I was about to close up and paid me three gold coins."

"Really?" Bev's brows rose. "That's awful kind of them."

"We actually sat around the table and had a cuppa. They wanted to know all about my mom and how long we'd had the bakery." He sighed happily. "First time I've really been able to talk about her at length."

Bev glanced at the top of the stairs, and not having heard the doors open yet, asked him, "They weren't wandering around Earl's workshop, were they?"

He shook his head. "No. Why?" He frowned. "Oh, Bev, you don't think... It was an accident, wasn't it?"

"Well, considering the culprits usually end up sleeping in my inn..." She shrugged. "They're almost a little *too* nice, you know?"

"How can someone be too nice, Bev?" Allen said. "You sound like Etheldra."

Before she could answer, the doors upstairs opened, and the three grannies came rushing down. They barely said hello to Allen before devouring the orange pastries, and it wasn't until they'd scarfed the last one that Bev realized she hadn't gotten one herself.

"That poor carpenter," Rita tutted.

"Does he need help rebuilding his workshop?" Janet asked.

Gladys dabbed her handkerchief against her lips. "We'd be happy to help."

"Oh, I'm sure he's got it," Bev said. If Earl didn't want the townsfolk helping him rebuild, he *definitely* didn't want these sweet, well-meaning ladies around.

"Nonsense, we're quite handy."

"Built a lot of workshops in my day."

"Why don't we pop over?"

"I really don't—" But before Bev could finish, the grannies were already halfway out the door. Bev let out a sigh. She had to see Earl anyway.

"See you later, Bev," Allen said, waving as Bev marched out the door, Biscuit happily trotting at her heels.

~

The grannies were nearly to the town square by the time Bev caught up with them. They didn't seem winded by their quick pace, either, which was surprising for a group their age.

"I know you guys mean well," Bev said, as she caught up with them. "Earl will have his shop rebuilt in a few weeks or so—"

"Then we'll expedite the process."

"Really, don't worry."

"Promise we know what we're doing."

"I'm sure you do, but you know how old carpenters are," Bev said, curious how the grannies knew which street to turn on to get to Earl's. "They're finicky."

"Oh, he'll just be happy it's done."

"They grouse, but they're grateful for the help."

"Don't worry, Bev, dear."

Despite Bev's best efforts, the grannies walked right up to the remains of Earl's workshop and started discussing how they'd rebuild it.

"What in the…" Earl had been on his back porch, stacking pieces of wood. "What are they doing here?"

"These ladies *insisted* on coming to see if they could help," Bev said, throwing her hands out apologetically. "I tried to stop them."

"No need to stop us, Bev," Janet said, picking up a nearby shovel and scooping up a large pile of ash. "We'll just get to work!"

"No time like the present," Gladys replied, bending over. "Oh, look. I found a piece of a hammer!"

"And I found a saw!" Rita said, waving the handle-less blade in the air.

"Er…" Earl rubbed the back of his head. "I suppose that's good. I'd borrowed some tools from folks in town, but nice to know my old pieces are still around. I'll need to get them down to the blacksmith to make new handles, I suppose, but..."

"Why don't we have that chat first, hm?" Bev said. "Then I can get these grannies back to the inn and out of your hair."

Bev followed Earl into his small house, which was just a single room. His twin bed was in the corner, and there was a small hearth with a kettle hanging over the fire. Bev could see why he always came to the Weary Dragon for dinner; there wasn't even a kitchen table.

Bev looked around. For a man who made chairs, there was a severe lack of them in his house—she spotted just one. "Um, where should I...?"

"Right there," he said, pointing at the lone seat. "I'll stand."

Bev plopped down as he handed her the tea. "Thanks."

"I don't have much in the way of food," he said apologetically. "Was just getting ready to come see you, actually."

"Not much in the way of food at the inn right now, either," Bev said. "Those ladies have some... uh...hearty appetites. Ate all Allen's pastries within a few minutes."

"I'm sure." He clasped his hands in front of him. "I'm glad you stopped by. What I want to say, I don't know... I just don't want it getting around until I know for sure."

"So you don't think it was an accident?" She

took a hesitant sip of the tea. Still too hot. "What do your neighbors say? Did they hear that explosion?"

He nodded. "Pip said he was in bed with the missus when he heard a loud bang. Gilda wasn't home yet, but her younger sister was—scared the poor dear half to death. She was white and shaking when I saw her."

"Valta?" Bev furrowed her brow. "She was just in my kitchen yesterday. Got into a scrap with Pip's boy and Vicky's brother. They had to clean flour out of my whole kitchen."

"Oh, that's who that third boy was, then. Vicky's brother," Earl said. "Thought he looked familiar but couldn't place him. The three of them were skulking around." He wiped his nose. "That's why I didn't want to say anything last night. I know Vicky and Allen are, well, not sure what to call them, exactly."

"Very good friends," Bev said. "I'm sure Allen wouldn't... if you *saw* them there..."

"I didn't see them there, exactly," Earl said. "I think they were over in Pip's yard, but they were close. I just wanted to mention it on the off chance... I'm sure they're good kids." He dropped his gaze, perhaps hoping Bev would fill in the blanks.

Bev wasn't in the habit of throwing around accusations, especially toward children. "Earl, I'm not sure..." she said after a long pause. "Even if they are responsible, it was probably an accident."

"Fires like that..." He cleared his throat. "I had a lot of wood in there, but as fast as it burned? That's not normal." He pushed the cup between his hands. "Now, I'm not saying it was those kids, but..."

"But?"

"But I had a few jugs of spirits in the shop." He held up his hands before Bev could react. "Not to drink, of course. I dissolve resin pieces in it to make varnish for the furniture. Now, I may be old, and my mind may be going a bit, but I do know there've been a few times when I've picked up one of the jugs and they've been a little *lighter* than usual. Can't say it was the kids, but..." He cleared his throat. "I've had to run them out of my shop a few times. Maybe been a bit too ornery with them. After a hard day's work, you get a little grumpy, too, I'd bet."

Bev wasn't sure she'd ever seen the old carpenter "grumpy."

"So you want me to talk with them?" she said with a heavy sigh.

"You said they'd gotten in trouble, right?" Earl said. "Maybe going to talk with their parents, you could... I don't know..." He lifted a shoulder. "See what they say?"

That was the *last* thing Bev wanted to do. People were funny about their kids, and Earl's suspicions were pretty light. But she'd told Earl she'd look into it.

"All right," she said. "I'll see what I can do."

"Thanks, Bev. I know this isn't what you signed up for, but you seem to be the only one in town who figures these things out." He rose with her and walked her to the door. "I'll see ol' Rustin, I'm sure. But…"

"Yeah, I know." Bev gave him the briefest of smiles. "Can't promise anything, but I'll do my best to—"

Her eyes widened as Earl opened the door. In the few minutes Bev and Earl had been talking, the grannies had cleaned up the rest of the ashy debris and set up a basic frame for the new workshop.

"What the…" Earl followed her outside, his eyebrows almost disappearing into his hairline. "How did you…?"

"I told you," Rita appeared from behind the shop with Earl's hammerhead in her hand. "We're quite good at rebuilding."

"Do it a lot," Janet said, walking out from the inside.

"We can't replace the woodworking, though," Gladys said. "So sorry you lost it all."

"But maybe you can get back to it sooner," Rita finished.

Janet nodded. "You're so talented."

Earl walked forward, still in shock. Bev,

however, kept her wary eyes on the grannies, wondering if maybe they were so adept at rebuilding because they were responsible for burning it down.

But she had no proof, other than a hunch, so with a groan, she turned on her heel and made her way toward Pip Norris's house.

Chapter Five

Pip and his wife Holly Norris were farriers who lived next door to Earl. Bev called on them every other month to reshoe Sin, and she liked them well enough. They had a quaint house with a neat front porch, and Bev held her breath as she climbed the stairs and knocked on the door.

Holly, a short, stocky woman, answered, a bright smile appearing on her face. "Good morning, Bev! Has Sin thrown her shoe again?"

"No, nothing like that," Bev said. "I…er…" Goodness, how did one go about doing this? "Well, Earl asked me to check with the neighbors to see if anyone saw anything last night. He's awful tore up about his warehouse."

"I know, poor thing." Holly opened the door wider to let Bev inside. "Come on in. I'll put on a kettle."

Bev wasn't in the mood for more tea but followed her inside anyway. The house was decorated with more flowery patterns than was to Bev's taste, but it was welcoming and well-loved. There was a sitting area with two chairs and a couch in front of the hearth, and a hallway that presumably led to bedrooms.

"Pip's already left for the day," she said, walking into the small kitchen area to grab the kettle. "But PJ is still asleep."

"Oh, is he?" Bev tried to look innocent. "Late night?"

"Well, with that fire next door, we were all up rather late," she said with a smile. "Why?"

"Just curious," she said, not wanting to bring up the flour incident or Earl's suspicions straight away. She focused her attention on the pressed flowers hanging on the wall as Holly finished up in the kitchen.

"There, should be ready in a jiffy," she said, sitting down across from Bev. "Now, what about that fire, eh?"

Bev nodded. "You didn't see anyone around beforehand, did you?"

"Can't say I did," she said. "Earl doesn't think someone started it on purpose, does he?"

"I think he's trying to explore every avenue," Bev said lightly. She folded her hands on her lap then unfolded them. "I wonder... Did PJ mention they'd come to the inn yesterday with the class?"

"No. No, he didn't," she said. "Hope you taught him something about baking and cleaning. Would be nice if he helped out around here more."

"So he didn't mention anything?" Bev asked.

She made a face. "Oh, goodness. What did he do?"

"It wasn't anything too bad," Bev said, holding up her hands. "They were there with Bardoff learning about baking and such and had a little too much fun with the flour. They cleaned it up nicely, though. Haven't seen the kitchen sparkle so much."

"I can't believe he didn't tell me." She pushed herself to stand. "I don't know what happened to my sweet boy. He was on my breast one minute, and now he's keeping secrets."

"I don't think..." Bev swallowed, considering her words. "Kids are kids, you know? He's a good boy, still."

"It's those two miscreants he started hanging out with. Valta Climber and Grant Hamblin. Ever since, I'm hearing he's been causing trouble all over town. The three of them were being loud yesterday." She paused, narrowing her gaze. "Surely, Earl doesn't think... That can't be why you're here, right?"

Bev hesitated. Should she be truthful or spare

the poor mother the grief? "Earl just asked me to check in with his neighbors and see if they heard or saw anything, that's all."

She sank back into the chair, shaking her head, but her tone was decidedly more guarded. "I didn't. We were in bed early. Only woke up because we heard the explosion."

"And what did the explosion sound like?" Bev asked.

"Like... well, an explosion, I suppose. Not sure I follow the question?"

Bev wasn't sure either. "I wish he'd just let Rustin handle this. I'm not really cut out for this kind of work."

"Aren't you, though?" She chuckled. "The sinkholes, the Harvest Festival, and I hear you were the lead actor in a huge kerfuffle over the solstice."

Holly had a point, but those hadn't involved her asking about townsfolks' kids. That seemed to be a new level of awkward.

"What in the...?" Holly was looking out the living room window at Earl's workshop. The grannies were on the roof, laying what appeared to be thatch. "Who in the world are they?"

"Three ladies who stayed at the inn last night," Bev said. "They insisted on helping, and before we even had a chance to decline, they had it back up."

"And Earl let them near his tools?" Holly snorted. "They must be pretty brave."

Beasts and Baking

Bev smiled thinly, following her gaze. "You didn't happen to…see *them* last night, did you?"

"Them? No, this is the first I've seen of them." She quirked a brow. "You don't think they set the fire then rebuilt the workshop, do you?"

"I don't think anyone *set* the fire intentionally," Bev said. "But accidents, you know. Earl said he has spirits in his workshop. Maybe someone knocked it over?"

"Hm." She smoothed the creases on her pants, glancing down the hall. "I wish I could help. But as I said, I was in bed early, as was my husband. And, of course, PJ, too." A nervous smile flitted across her face, and Bev could practically hear the conversation she'd have with her son later. "You know, I've got to get over to Alice's to reshoe her horse, so…"

"Right, of course." Bev rose quickly. Suppose that cuppa was all but forgotten. "Sorry to take up your time this morning. But if you remember anything, or PJ does—"

"I'll be sure to tell Earl."

The Norrises were good people, and if PJ was involved, his parents would certainly hold his feet to the fire about it. But coming clean to Earl would be another story.

Still, it was clear he hadn't been the only one skulking around, so Bev decided she'd make a day of asking awkward questions, just to get it all out of the way. Instead of traveling out to the country to meet with the Climbers, who she didn't know very well, she headed for the blacksmith's shop, where she'd find Valta's sister Gilda at work. It was directly across from Earl's house, and Bev could see the grannies working from inside.

The older Climber sister was nearing the end of her apprenticeship and would have to make the decision to stay in Pigsend or try to make her way in another town needing her skills.

She and Gore Dewey, her mentor, were the primary sources of farm equipment in town. Their shop was filled with scythes and hoes and shovels—not to mention nails, hammers, wheel parts, horseshoes, and whatever else was needed of metal in Pigsend. Bev called on her for candlesticks for the inn and was hoping to do better at *not* offending her.

Bev found the apprentice hammering a white-hot piece of metal, wearing an outfit made of leather and a steel mask. Bev winced as the hammer struck the metal, sending sparks across the room. She waited until Gilda plunged the metal into the nearby barrel of water before ringing the bell at the front.

"Oh, Bev!" Gilda popped up the mask, revealing a wide smile and freckles smattered across her cheeks. She gave Vellora a run for her money in muscles but wasn't nearly as tall. "What can I do for you today?"

"Morning, Gilda," Bev said, forcing a smile onto her face. "Just wanted to check on your sister, actually. Is she all right?"

"On account of the flour incident yesterday?" Gilda rolled her eyes.

Well, at least one of the kids had been forthcoming. "That, and also, I heard she was pretty shaken up by the explosion over at Earl's place."

"She was over there?" Gilda frowned. "I swear, that kid's become a magnet for trouble."

"I think she was with her friends, the Norris boy and Grant Hamblin."

"Of course she was." Gilda scoffed. "You know, those boys are trouble. Never had a problem with Valta until she started spending her after-school time with them. Been trying to get her interested in blacksmithing, but she'll run out the moment I stoke the fires." She shook her head as she removed the now-cool metal object from the water. It was a shovel. "In any case, I haven't seen her this morning. Have half a mind to walk over to that school and pull her out. My folks don't know why they keep sending her there when there's work to be done at the farm. Already mad at *me* for leaving."

Bev remembered what Bardoff had said about the kids disappearing as they got older. "I think the school is good for her. The three of them cleaned the kitchen up very well, I have to say. Just got carried away, as kids do."

"You're too kind, Bev. Sometimes, kids need a bit of sense knocked into them." She waved the shovel then stopped, looking bashful.

"Look, if you talk to Valta this afternoon, ask her if she saw anything. Anything she might remember could be helpful."

Gilda lifted a brow. "Oh? Are you sleuthing again?"

"Not by choice. Earl asked me to..." She considered her words. "Well, he said the kids were nearby earlier in the evening."

"And he probably thinks they caused it, too."

"I didn't say that."

"You didn't have to." Gilda sighed. "I'll see what I can wheedle out of her. But if it *was* her..." She shook her head. "She's just a kid, you know? Would hate to see her throw away her future because of one mistake."

"No one's saying anything about punishment," Bev said. "I'm sure Earl would ask them maybe to help him rebuild, or—"

"Looks like those old ladies are doing a good enough job of that," Gilda said, nodding to Janet, who was on the roof of the workshop. "Can't believe how fast they've got that thing back up. Practically a miracle. Maybe *they're* the ones doing the burning, eh?"

"I've certainly considered it," Bev said.

Having spoken with two of the three kids' guardians and having gotten pretty much the same reaction from them, Bev walked up to Apolinary's seamstress shop with trepidation. She and Vicky got along well, especially since the assistant had started seeing Allen romantically, but Bev had gotten along with the others as well and had left with a decidedly icky feeling after today's conversations.

"Oh, hey, Bev," Vicky said, not looking too pleased to see her. "Come on in. Do you need something mended?"

"No, I was actually—"

"Coming to ask if I punished Grant for ruining your kitchen?" She shook her head. "I'm so sorry. He's been a mess ever since he started hanging out with those other two miscreants." She put down the skirt she was working on. "I've told him he's to come straight home after school for the next two weeks."

Bev chuckled as she approached the counter slowly. "Did he come straight home last night?"

"He was home after dinner, but I figured you'd kept him late at the inn," she said. "What did he do now?"

"Nothing at all," Bev said. "That I know of, anyway. But Earl said he saw Grant and his friends near his shop before the explosion."

"I ain't seen nothing." Grant appeared from the

backroom, his face a mask of fury. "And neither did my friends. That old man is just making up stories."

"Grant," Vicky said with a warning glance. "I thought you said you were sick. Supposed to be lying down in the back."

"I saw Bev coming and knew she was here to ask questions. That's her thing now, you know." He pointed an accusatory finger at Bev. "How do we know *you* didn't start the fire?"

"Because I was in a room full of people, including Earl, when it happened," Bev said.

"Well, if Earl was there, how does he know my brother and his friends were in his backyard?" Vicky asked.

"I didn't say they were in his backyard, just that they were in the Norrises's." Bev turned to Grant. "I wanted to ask if you saw anything out of the ordinary. I asked the same of Earl's other neighbors."

"Oh." He shifted. "No. I didn't."

"Grant." Vicky turned to him. "Don't you dare lie to Bev."

"I'm not lying!" he cried, sounding very much like he was. "We were in PJ's backyard. Never set foot on the old man's property."

"When did you leave PJ's?" Bev asked.

"I dunno. Sunset?" He seemed agitated as he twisted in his own skin. "Right, Vicky?"

"I was…er…wasn't home until later last night,"

Vicky said, her cheeks turning pink. Bev could only assume she was with Allen. "But Grant, if you started that fire—"

"I told you, we didn't do a thing," he said, his face turning blotchy as he turned to Bev. "And you got a lot of nerve coming in here and accusing—"

"I'm not accusing anyone of anything," Bev said. "But you seem awfully tetchy for someone who's completely innocent."

"Because that old man has it out for us!" Grant huffed. "Everyone always thinks we're up to no good. We're just hanging around."

"They probably think you're up to no good precisely *because* you're just *hanging around*," Vicky said. "You need to get a job, Grant. Idle hands and all that. I'm not going to be around forever to take care of you and put a roof over your head, so—"

Grant scoffed but said nothing.

"I know that's why Bardoff has the kids visiting all the shops in the area," Bev said, trying to ease out of the family squabble. "Perhaps something will pique his interest."

"Not likely," the teen grumbled.

"Well, in the meantime," Bev smoothed her shirt, "the question is simple: Did you three see anything strange at Earl's when you were in PJ's backyard?"

"No. We didn't." He folded his arms across his chest. "There, happy?"

"Very." She turned to Vicky, who'd been watching her brother with a narrow gaze. "Vicky, sorry to interrupt your day."

"No problem at all, Bev." She forced a smile. "I hope Earl gets his place rebuilt soon. I know it meant a lot to him."

"It…uh…" Bev glanced at the door. "Well, it got rebuilt already, it seems. Some handy folks staying at the inn offered to help. Won't replace what was inside, though." She caught Grant's gaze. "He'd spent all winter making those chairs. Probably going to take him a few months to get it all back, what with his workload growing with spring…"

"Maybe shoulda kept his spirits locked up, then," Grant said with a huff before disappearing back through the curtain.

"If it was him, I'll find out," Vicky said. "And he'll be working off the debt to Earl until it's satisfied." She paused. "Maybe I'll volunteer him anyway. Would be good to keep him away from the other two. They always seem to get him in trouble."

"Seems to be a theme. So…" She leaned on the table. "Late night with Allen?"

"None of your business," she squeaked, but based on the smile that threatened to explode on her face, she'd had a lovely night, indeed. "Why don't you keep your attention on Earl, hm? My brother and his friends can't be your only suspects, can they?"

Bev didn't have the heart to tell her they were. "A few other ideas."

"What all did Earl have in that shop?" Vicky asked, sitting down and picking up the skirt again. "Maybe someone wanted to burn *that* down and took the workshop with it."

"Only one I know for sure was Mayor Hendry," Bev said. "But that seems a bit excessive, don't you think?"

"Depends on how mad someone is with Mayor Hendry," Vicky said. "If I were you, I'd ask Earl who else he was making furniture for. Maybe there's someone with a vendetta." She glanced at the back room. "I'll keep the screws to Grant. If he was in any way responsible, I'll be sure to let you know." She stabbed the skirt. "He's a good kid, but he needs to learn he's fast approaching adulthood. And one day…" She licked her lips. "One day, I might just have my own life to lead."

Chapter Six

After spending most of the morning having awkward conversations with townsfolk, Bev was happy to walk into the butcher shop. Ida was manning the front counter while Vellora worked in the back, and both seemed pleased to see Bev.

"We went up to Earl's to help, but...uh...your lovely guests seem to have it under control," Ida said. "They'd already gotten the roof and most of the walls up."

"Where did you say they came from?" Vellora asked.

"They didn't say. But I'm glad they were around to lend a hand."

"How goes the investigation?" Ida asked. "Do

you have anything juicy to share with us?"

"Hardly," Bev said. "And I wouldn't call it an investigation quite yet. Just trying to see if anyone saw anything. So far…nothing."

"I'm sure you'll find some clue or small detail that unravels the entire thing," Ida said with a sigh. "After all, if it wasn't for you, we'd probably be sitting in a prison."

"Or a hundred-fifty gold coins poorer," Vellora added.

"I didn't do… Well, Bernie revealed himself. I only brought the players together," Bev said, waving her hand. She was happier to forget the whole solstice incident had happened, but the butchers seemed to recall it with fonder memories. "And the Harvest Festival—"

"Was all you," Ida said. "You're the one who found the proof in Claude's room."

"Biscuit found it," Bev said.

"Oh, stop being so modest." Ida wiped down the counter absentmindedly. "And just *spill*. I want to know what you've found."

"I told you, not much," Bev said. "Earl thought he saw some kids near his yard before it went up in flames, but they weren't forthcoming."

"Which kids?" Vellora asked.

"Vicky's brother, the Norris boy, and Gilda's sister," Bev said.

"Yeah, I've seen them skulking around town

together," Ida said. "Or, well, they *look* like they're causing trouble."

"How does one *look* like they're causing trouble?" Bev asked.

"You know." She shrugged. "Loitering. Snickering. Talking amongst themselves. You know, miscreant stuff."

"I hardly think standing around laughing is problematic," Vellora said.

"No, but they're the only teenagers in town who don't have jobs," Ida said. "Idle hands and whatever that saying is."

"Vicky said the same thing," Bev said. "Grant was the only one I got to speak with directly, and he sure didn't act innocent. His sister said she'd put pressure on him, but something tells me that's not going to work. Seems like they're in something of a tiff at the moment. Vicky kept talking about him needing to support himself."

"Well, I should say so!" Ida said. "Fourteen and not even interested in a trade? At his age, I'd already been working in the shop alongside my father for years. Glad I did—can't imagine how I would've struggled to keep this business afloat had I not learned all I could from him before he and my mother died."

"I suppose that's important, too," Bev said. "Bardoff is hoping to expose the kids to all manner of occupations—both in and out of town. I think he's hoping they'll broaden their horizons to be more than just farmers."

"And that's a nice dream for someone with the wherewithal to leave Pigsend and study in a faraway school," Ida said. "But the kids around here? They're gonna end up in the same industries as their parents. And that's a good thing. Because if all the kids left to go be scholars, who'd be our farriers? Our blacksmiths? Our—"

"Butchers?" Bev prompted, earning a bashful look from Ida.

"Well…" She cleared her throat. "Okay, maybe I'm projecting a little. But the point remains: they need to be doing something useful or this isn't the last fire they'll set."

"*Allegedly* set," Bev said. "Remember, no one saw anything."

"So Grant says," Ida said. "But why would he rat out his friends?"

"I will say, Vicky's brother's always been a bit snotty to me," Vellora said. "She puts up with a lot from him, in my opinion."

"She doesn't really have much of a choice, you know," Ida said. To Bev's confused face, she explained, "Their mom died during the dragon pox epidemic, and their father left to…well, he told his kids he'd be back after he made his fortunes in the war."

"Did he?" Bev asked.

"No one's heard from him. Didn't show up on the rolls, either," Ida said, glancing at Vellora, who had that faraway look in her eye she got whenever someone mentioned the bloody war between the kingside and queenside.

"You think he'd abandon his family like that?" Vellora asked.

"I think..." Ida shrugged. "I think he wasn't making much of himself here. From what I understand, it was something of a scandal that he married Ashla. She came from money, and threw it all away for *love*. But I guess her family was right after all, since he left their children in the lurch. Thank goodness for Apolinary."

"Yeah?" Bev asked. "Why?"

"Well, when Rosie Kelooke retired, Apolinary was in need of an assistant. She took Vicky under her wing. Rented her the apartment for a deep discount, too. Girl was barely sixteen at the time, and her brother wasn't yet ten."

"I wonder why Vicky's ready to kick him out, then?" Bev asked.

"Well, I would think it's obvious," Vellora said with a knowing smile. "I assume she thinks she's going to be a bride soon."

"Oh, you're probably right, Vel," Ida said. "Nobody wants their little brother hanging around when they're enjoying marital bliss."

"Somebody had better tell Allen, then," Bev

said. "He hasn't said a word about it to me."

"Me neither," Ida said with a shake of her head. "But I suppose we'll all hear about it when it happens."

"If it happens," Vellora said, watching the bakery across the street. "Allen might just chicken out."

"We won't let him, will we, Bev?" Ida said, her eyes going wistful. "Oh, how wonderful it would be to have another wedding in town."

"I'd certainly like the business," Bev said.

"Too true," Ida said. "Speaking of, those old ladies you're hosting are something else, aren't they?"

"Have you met them?" Bev asked.

Ida nodded. "When we stopped in at Earl's, they paid us *two* extra gold coins so we'd double whatever you'd ordered for dinner. Said you were practically *starving* them."

"That's an exaggeration," Bev said. "There was nearly a pound of meat per person last night!"

"Well, now there'll be two," Ida said with a chuckle.

"You know, I've half a mind to think *they* burned down the warehouse," Bev said.

"And rebuilt it?" Vellora laughed. "That seems unlikely."

"Unlikelier things have happened, especially in this town." Bev rapped her fingers on the counter.

"Vicky thought I should ask Earl who else he was making furniture for. Maybe someone wanted revenge."

"Or maybe she just wanted you to stop asking about her brother," Vellora said.

"I'm sure, but it's worth looking into if Earl thinks someone set it intentionally." Bev shrugged. "At least until I can get something else out of the kids."

"Who are we to argue? You are the *expert*," Ida said with a giggle. "Boy, who'da thought Bev would turn into our resident detective?"

"We do have a sheriff." Bev made a face. "Where is he, anyway? Didn't see him at the fire or around town today."

"Maybe that's another mystery for you to solve," Vellora said. "The Disappearance of Sheriff Rustin."

"Har har." Bev glared at them both. "Seriously, have either of you seen him?"

"Not since we've been back." Ida waved off Bev's concern. "Oh, I'm sure he's fine. Probably on a little holiday. Sheriffs deserve that every so often."

"Even ones that don't do much around town," Vellora added.

"I suppose." Bev shrugged. "Did the grannies give you their preference for meat?"

"I've got it almost ready for you," Vellora said. "Might take you a couple trips, though."

"I'll help," Ida said with a wink.

There was a *lot* of meat—roughly the same amount Bev ordered for the Harvest Festival nights. That three old ladies could put all this food away was another curiosity Bev couldn't get out of her head, but thus far…well, it didn't seem to warrant investigating. They'd rebuilt Earl's warehouse, they'd paid gold coins to the butchers and the baker for the extra food, and they'd just been as nice as could be to Bev and everyone else. The only thing Bev had to complain about was she'd had to break out her large pots and pans.

At exactly six o'clock, Bev brought out dinner, and as expected, the grannies were ready with their plates and forks. Earl, Etheldra, and Bardoff were behind them, watching with a mixture of scrutiny and amusement.

"Got enough food, there, Bev?" Etheldra asked as Bev hoisted the platter onto the table.

"Oh, that's mostly for us, dearie," Janet said.

"We asked the butchers to double the order," Rita replied.

"Really?" Etheldra gave them a look. "You're going to eat all this food?"

"And how!" Gladys said, shoveling large pieces of beef onto her plate. They took more than half of the meat, but as there was so much, there was plenty for the three locals to share—and all of the rosemary bread.

"Oh, we're not much for the bread and grains," Rita said.

"No?" Etheldra waved around her own piece. "But this bread's won awards."

"We're big meat-eaters," Gladys replied.

"Always have been. Just something delicious about a seared piece of meat." Janet took a large bite of the beef. "Outstanding, Bev."

"Suppose you've built up an appetite, what with rebuilding Earl's workhouse," Etheldra said, her voice sharp and clear. "Just so kind of you to do it. Amazed you have the skills."

"Oh, when you live as long as we have, you do find yourself learning different things," Gladys said.

"But you're...well, you're old," Etheldra said.

"So are you, Etheldra," Bev said with a look.

"Yes, and I'm not rebuilding workshops in a matter of hours," she replied with a thin smile.

"We're younger than we look." Janet glanced around at the mostly empty plates. "Has everyone had enough? Mind if we finish off the rest?"

Nobody said anything to the contrary, so the three grannies rose and helped themselves to more meat and potatoes, and still none of the bread. Etheldra stared at them then turned to Bev as if expecting Bev to say something about it. But she just shrugged. They were allowed to eat as much as they wanted, especially as they'd paid extra for the privilege.

Beasts and Baking

Earl, who'd been quiet most of the evening, was the first to finish his plate, and brought it to Bev with a tight smile. "How did… How did it go today? Chatting with the neighbors?"

Bev felt Etheldra's beady eyes on her. The last thing Bev wanted was the taciturn tea-shop owner performing another *interrogation* of her own, as she'd done during the solstice. Although the grannies seemed impervious to her bluntness, Bev doubted the Norrises or Vicky or Gilda would take too kindly to the tea shop owner's bluntness. Nor did Bev think Etheldra could get more out of them than Bev had. Probably better to keep things closer to the vest.

"Why don't we step into the kitchen, Earl?" Bev said.

Earl followed her inside, and Biscuit sat by the door, as if he knew to listen for eavesdroppers. Not that Bev was harboring a closely guarded secret, but she did prefer this conversation to happen in private.

She offered Earl the other stool against her kitchen table, but he declined, holding his hat between his hands as if he'd done something wrong.

"So?" He gripped his hat tighter. "What'd you find out?"

"Spoke with Holly, Gilda, and Vicky," Bev said. "They all swear their kids weren't in your backyard."

His gray eyebrows narrowed quickly. "Then they're lying. I *saw* them there."

"Earl, you were here at the inn when the explosion happened," Bev said with a frustrated sigh. "Remember? So you can't say definitively if they were there or not."

"But surely you found something that..." Earl cleared his throat. "Someone *set* that fire, Bev."

"To what end?" Bev asked.

He frowned, thinking for a moment. "Well, I don't know. If it was those kids, probably just to cause trouble—"

"But what if it wasn't the kids?" Bev asked. "What if it was someone else entirely?"

He paused. "I don't follow."

"If you think it was set intentionally, maybe it's worth asking what the target was." Bev sat on her stool. "Is there anyone in town who thinks you've wronged them?"

He shook his head. "Not to my knowledge, no."

She hadn't thought so, but the question had to be asked. "Then who else were you making furniture for?"

He bristled. "Hardly see why that's relevant."

"There's a chance someone set the fire to get back at someone," Bev said. "If not you, then maybe someone you were making furniture for."

"That's ridiculous. It's *furniture*." Earl scoffed. "I thought you were gonna take this seriously, Bev? After all I've..." He stopped. "Well, I just thought you'd help me. But if I was wrong—"

"I *am* helping, Earl." She crossed the room to put a comforting hand on his arm. "But unless you have someone who said they saw the three kids actually *set* the fire, there's really nothing else I can do. We can't just blindly accuse them of something when we don't have proof. That's not fair."

"Suppose not," he said. "But I just *know* they had something to do with it."

"I promise I'm not letting them off the hook," Bev said. "And the moment I find something that puts them in your workshop when the fire started, I'll be sure to tell you. But in the meantime, I have to keep exploring other options, just in case there's something we're missing. Sometimes, the answers aren't clear until you start looking at all possible scenarios." She squeezed his arm. "Trust me on this, okay? I've done this a few times now."

He gave her a half-smile. "Sorry, Bev. I'm just not used to being the focus of these things. Looking at them from afar, it seems like you just fix everything."

"Well, I'm not promising I'll fix anything." Bev sighed as she sat back down on her stool. "But I do need to know who else had furniture in your workshop."

"Hendry had a set of chairs," he said, counting off on his fingers. "I was also working on something for Bathilda, but that wasn't in the shop, and a couple of picture frames for Ramone and their brother." He sighed, shaking his head. "All that work, gone. I didn't have a chance to really think about it until I walked into the empty workshop this evening." His eyes grew misty. "Just hours and hours of work. Makes me tired thinking about having to redo it all."

Bev had no words of comfort for that. "Was the shop rebuilt to your standards?"

"And then some," he said. "Not that I coulda told them otherwise if it hadn't been. They're awfully pushy. Nice as they can be, but pushy."

"I can see that," Bev said.

"Told me to kick my feet up and relax while they did all the work." He pushed his cap up as he scratched his forehead. "I'm grateful to 'em for doing it. Can't imagine how far behind I'd be if I were still framing it in. I swear, Mayor Hendry came by three times today to see when those chairs would be ready."

"The ones that..." Bev let out a frustrated sigh. "She knows they were burnt up, right?"

"She's insistent."

Interesting. "Do you know what she's using them for?"

"Sitting, I reckon." He smiled. "You know the mayor. She likes things done on her time. I told her I'd work on them as quick as I can."

"Not too quickly," Bev said. "It's been a hard couple of days for you, Earl. You should take a few days and relax. Let the mayor fret about her chairs."

"You know I can't do that. Not in my nature." He pulled his cap back on. "You have a good night, Bev. Be sure to take care of those ladies. Goodness knows they took care of my shop today." He slipped out the back door and into the night.

Bev stood with her hands on her hips, looking down at her laelaps.

"Well, Biscuit, I guess we're going to pay Mayor Hendry a visit tomorrow."

Chapter Seven

In the morning, Bev sped through her chores, her mind on how she would approach Hendry and what she might say. The mayor had a habit of ending conversations she didn't want to be part of, and Bev needed to ensure she had all her wits about her.

"Biscuit, do you want to go for a walk?" Bev asked as she wrapped up the rest of her chores.

The laelaps rose slowly from his splayed-out position near the fire and yawned in an overly dramatic fashion, letting out a low yelp.

"Take your time," Bev muttered.

With the small dog at her heels, Bev headed toward Hendry's office in the town hall building. It

Beasts and Baking

sat in the middle of Pigsend, facing the schoolhouse and library. The large square in front had once held a magnificent dragon fountain, but it had been the first casualty of the sinkholes some months ago. Ramone Comely had said they were making another, but Bev hadn't heard about any progress since the winter. But Earl had mentioned he was making picture frames for the sculptor and their painter brother, so Bev would probably be paying them a visit later.

The hall was the site of town meetings, and though it had been a while since Pigsend had gathered to complain about this or that, Bev wasn't eager to have another one. Lately, these meetings resulted in Bev getting hauled up in front of the group to answer questions about sinkholes or Harvest Festivals. Hopefully, Earl's fire was the first and last of them, and Bev wouldn't have to sit for hours discussing all the theories of who could've been behind it.

She hoped.

The mayor was at her desk, reading through papers with a slight wrinkle in her otherwise-perfect face. She had porcelain-white skin and jet-black hair, and always had a perfect shade of blood red on her lips. Her hawklike gaze snapped up as soon as Bev darkened her doorway, and she unfurled a smile like a cat stretching in the sun.

"If it isn't my favorite innkeeper," she said.

"What can I do for you, Bev? Oh." She wrinkled her nose as Biscuit bounded in after Bev. "You brought the dog."

"Biscuit, sit," Bev said, and surprisingly, the laelaps plopped his butt down beside her, even though his nose was twitching toward the mayor.

"I would *rather* he stay outside," Hendry drawled. "I'm terribly allergic."

"Are you now?" Bev quirked a brow. "Never mentioned it before."

As if proving a point, Hendry let out a loud (and possibly fake) sneeze.

"Fine." Bev nodded to Biscuit. "Go sit outside, please."

The laelaps let out a low ruff but did as instructed, his white-tipped tail disappearing out the front of the town hall.

Bev went to turn back, but before she could, she noticed the sheriff's office across the hall was dark. "Where's Rustin?"

"Oh, our dear sheriff is taking some much-needed time off," she said, keeping a wary eye on the door, as if waiting for the dog to come back in. "Though perhaps he should've picked a better time. Can't believe someone set fire to poor Earl's workshop."

Bev went to sit, but there wasn't a place to do that anymore. "What happened to the chairs that were in here?"

"Why do you think I asked Earl for those chairs to be made so quickly?" Hendry said with a knowing smile. "Can't have people standing in my office willy-nilly."

"Why'd you get rid of the old ones?" Bev asked. "They were fine, weren't they?"

"Decent enough." She clicked her tongue. "But not fit for a mayor, in my view. Need to be worthy of all the queen's folk we have passing through town recently."

Bev didn't see how chairs would be "fit" for anything.

"I take it you're on the case again?" Hendry asked with a smile.

"I'm not…" Bev sighed. "Rustin *really* should be the one doing the investigating."

"Yes, but you're so good at it."

"Then maybe we should get a better sheriff."

"Bev, darling, you don't *want* a better sheriff," Hendry said, sitting back in her chair as her eyes sparkled with amusement. "What, a Dag Flanigan-type who'll arrest anyone with the slightest hint of magic?" She twirled in her chair. "I don't think the butchers would like that sort of pressure, do you?"

I'd wager you wouldn't either, the way Biscuit was sniffing you. "Fine, we'll keep him. But honestly, I need to start collecting a salary if I'm going to keep doing all this extra work."

"I'll see about getting you a medal. Now…" She

clapped her hands and leaned forward. "What have you discovered about poor Earl's workshop?"

"Nothing. Earl thinks it was the local hooligans, the hooligans aren't saying much, and the only other thing I've got is to see if anyone he was making furniture for was the real target."

"The real target. How your imagination flies!" She picked up a piece of paper and read it. "Look, Bev, I think we *all* think it was *probably* the kids, right? So I think we just tell their parents and guardians they'll be required to work for Earl until the debt is satisfied and be done with it."

"We?" Bev chuckled. "Who's we?"

"You, obviously, since you're the one investigating."

"Well, *we* don't know that," Bev said. "Which is why I'm here. Is there a chance someone burned down Earl's warehouse to get to you?"

She laughed. "Bev, who in their right mind would think destroying a pair of half-finished chairs would *get to* me?"

"I don't know. That's why I'm asking."

"No, Bev. I don't *have* enemies. If I did, I wouldn't be in office, would I?"

"That's not—"

"Bev, I'm quite busy, so if that's all…"

~

The next thing Bev knew, she was walking down the street to the Weary Dragon, without much memory of how she'd gotten there. Biscuit was steadfastly by her side, watching her with concern in his golden eyes. When she caught his gaze, he wagged his tail happily.

"What in the—?" Bev spun around, glaring at the clock tower in the distance. No wonder Hendry was content with Rustin as her law enforcement. It would've been hard to hide her magical manipulations from someone like Dag Flanigan, the ruthless magic-hunter who'd come to town during the solstice. Bev had been grateful he'd been in town to stop Bernie from swindling the Witzels but was happy he moved on without doing any *more* investigating.

"I can't say the mayor isn't involved with the fire in some way," Bev said to Biscuit. "But we'll put it in our back pocket for now."

Bev walked by the inn and kept going. Ramone lived a few doors down, and since she was asking questions, might as well keep at it.

It was a much faster walk than the last time she'd been here, when there'd been a few feet of snow on the ground, and everyone had been stuck in town. The artist had been a secondary player in the chaos, as their brother had been secretly staying at the inn. It had all come to light and, thanks to a bit of empath magic, the two had reconciled. Horst was still staying with Ramone, it seemed, so the push from the magic seemed to be permanent.

"Oh, Bev!" Ramone opened the door with a large grin on their face. Dressed in a vibrant green tunic and dark brown pants, they opened the door wider to allow Bev to see inside.

"This looks…" Bev couldn't believe her eyes. When she'd last been there, the room had been a mess of small dragon figurines with a single seating area. Now, everything was gone, save a large block of stone in the center of the room that was starting to grow wings. "Wow. You're working on the fountain?"

"I am, I am," they said, clapping their hands. "Oh, it's going to be magnificent, Bev. You just wait and see. I'm hoping to be done by the spring."

"Where in the world did you get this stone?" Bev asked. "And how did you get it here?"

"My dear brother was helpful. Called in some favors from some friends in Middleburg." They called out, "Horst? Are you up there? Bev's here for a visit!"

Ramone's brother appeared behind the large rock. Bev had known him as The Mysterious H when he'd stayed at the Weary Dragon, a grumpy, anti-social sort of person who was eager to leave and more eager to keep his presence under wraps. Seeing him with a bright smile was still a little strange to Bev, but she was happy the two were getting along.

"I actually had a couple questions for you," Bev said. "I'm sure you heard about Earl's warehouse, right?"

"We did," Ramone said with a solemn nod. "Just an absolute shame. Wonder what happened?"

"Earl thinks someone set it intentionally," Bev said. "And we heard an explosion, too."

"Oh, we heard that, too, didn't we?" Ramone said. "Scared me half to death the other night."

"Who does he think is responsible?" Horst asked.

Bev didn't think it pertinent to mention the kids. "No one. Asked me to look into it since—"

"You're the resident detective?" Ramone said with a grin.

She lifted a shoulder. "That's what they tell me."

"So what questions do you have for us?" Horst asked.

"Well, I know Earl was making picture frames for you," Bev said. "Any chance someone set the warehouse on fire to get to you?"

Horst chuckled, and Ramone shook their head. "Oh, who'd want to get to us, Bev? We're artists."

"You never know," Bev said. "Was there anything special about the frames you'd asked him to make?"

"Just wanted them to be big enough to hold Horst's art. We were going to travel to Middleburg to sell them in the spring." Ramone beamed at their brother. "Hope to fetch a good price for them."

"I take it the gig at Kaiser Tuckey is no longer

on the table?" Bev asked.

"Well, I just feel so much more creative here," Horst said. "And it's been nice to reconnect with my sibling."

A traveling clergyman with some empath and persuasive powers (not unlike Mayor Hendry) had said the siblings tapped into some kind of magic being together.

"No bad blood with Kaiser?" Bev asked.

Horst shook his head. "He was pleased we were both making art again and invited us to come visit any time if we make anything he might enjoy."

Dead end there. "Was there anything suspicious about Earl's workshop? Anyone around you remember seeing who looked strange?"

"Not that I remember," Horst said. "Ramone?"

The sculptor tapped their chin thoughtfully. "Now that you mention it, when we were giving Earl our dimensions, Mayor Hendry stopped by. Acted rather rude, if I recall. Gave Earl a bag and told him to use *that* on her chairs."

"Was it paint?"

"No, it looked like amber chips of some kind," Ramone said.

"Probably resin," Horst said.

Bev nodded. Earl had said he dissolved sap from trees in alcohol to finish off the furniture. "I can't imagine why she'd be annoyed you were there."

"Oh, you know the mayor. She's always up to

something." Ramone waved the air. "She was probably just mad I haven't delivered the statue she'd paid for last year."

Bev glanced at the unfinished stone art. "She'll be happy with this, I'm sure. Anything else you remember?"

"No, sorry, Bev." Ramone smiled. "But if I do, I'll be sure to pop by the inn."

"Might pop by anyway, if you're making that rosemary bread," Horst said with a grin.

"Every night, until it gets too hot," Bev said. "But you'd better come early. I've got a trio of folks staying there who like to eat."

"Oh, those old dears?" Ramone shared a look with their brother. "How lovely. They stopped in recently. Had heard about the statue and wanted to see it for themselves."

Bev started. *Here, too?* "They certainly do get around." She rose. "Anything else you remember about Mayor Hendry and Earl?"

"Only that she told him to use *that* on her chairs, and *only that*," Horst said, mimicking Hendry's tone. "And she'd know if he didn't."

Once again, Bev bypassed the Weary Dragon (she had time…probably) and headed straight for Earl's warehouse. There was something to be said about being forgetful, but that Earl hadn't mentioned Hendry's odd request at all was puzzling.

Earl was putting the finishing touches on the cabinets lining the walls. The workshop interior still smelled like sawdust, and Bev had to agree the grannies had done a good job with construction.

Construction, art, baking—they certainly have a variety of talents.

"Oh, hey, Bev," Earl said, turning as she made her presence known. "Just finishing these cabinets up. Headed to Middleburg in the morning to get some more wood. Gilda's going to refashion some of my tools. Found the iron in the ashes. Thank goodness that doesn't burn, eh?"

"Yes, thank goodness." She tilted her head. "Say, Earl. Was there anything special about the furniture that burned up?"

"You already asked me that, Bev," he said with a chuckle. "I told you no."

"What about Mayor Hendry's chairs?"

"Nope."

Bev pursed her lips. "What about the special resin she wanted put on the chairs?"

He shrugged but didn't quite look her in the eye. "Yeah? People have preferences. She dropped it off. Can't see why it was worth mentioning."

"May I see it?" she asked, taking a step toward him.

"Got destroyed." He gestured to the empty workshop. "Everything did."

Bev quirked a brow. "Everything? Then why is

she so keen on you remaking the chairs?"

He hemmed and hawed for a moment, before clearing his throat loudly. "Might you be looking at those kids, Bev? They knocked something over. I'm sure of it."

"Earl." Bev put a hand on his shoulder. "You can tell me. It's all right. You know I won't judge."

He sighed. "I don't know if there is anything *to* tell, really. But I know I can't be blabbing other people's secrets. Like how often I gotta fix bed frames because two folks got a bit too excited doin' their business." He chuckled. "If people thought I was going around town, flapping my jaws about this and that, they'd never hire me again."

"I'm just trying to find out who might've burned down your workshop," Bev said gently. "But if you'd rather I didn't—"

"No, no…" He sighed. "Well, I'm not exactly sure what was so special about it, except it was. Hendry said it was *this* specific resin she wanted put on the chairs, and she'd know if I used something else. Was real funny about it, too." He paused, taking a breath, reaching into his newly created cabinet and pulling out a small jug. "Not sure what kinda sap it is, but when I started using it on the chairs, it made me feel a funny way."

Bev peered inside, the pungent odor of spirits tickling her nostrils and making her a little dizzy.

No, not just dizzy. There seemed to be

something else. Something *magical*. It gave her that same fuzzy-headed feeling as when Hendry had spelled her earlier that day. The mayor seemed to have infused her own magic in the resin. For what purpose?

If she had any doubts about her own senses, Biscuit was keenly interested in the solution, his nose twitching as he stood on his hind legs, trying to get at whatever was in the jug.

"I don't think this is something that's really worth much discussion," Earl said. "Especially with the mayor. Don't think she'd take too kindly to you making accusations about what she can and can't do."

"Wouldn't dream of it," Bev said. "Was there anyone else who dropped off something weird?"

"No. Bathilda had been by earlier to pay for the fence I'd built her. But—"

"Earl!" A voice called from beyond the workshop. Alice Estrich, a farmer who lived on the west side of town, came dashing into the workshop. "Earl, you have to come quickly."

"Alice? What's wrong?" Bev asked.

"It's my barn. It's been... It's been completely destroyed!"

Chapter Eight

Alice's farm was a twenty-minute walk from Earl's place, and even before they reached her property, bits of her destroyed barn littered the dirt road. She didn't seem physically hurt but definitely looked shaken.

"I can't even… Looks like a nasty storm blew it away," she said, almost babbling. "But there's not a cloud in the sky today. And nothing else was destroyed. Never seen anything like it."

"What were you doing when it happened?" Bev asked.

"I'd just been out tending to the animals," Alice replied. "Came back inside for a spot of lunch. And all of a sudden…*boom!* I saw the barn collapse from the kitchen window. Then it started raining wood and debris. Big cloud of smoke."

"So it's on fire?" Bev asked.

"No." She shook her head. "It was like...I don't know, a big gust of wind came and blew it apart or something."

"And you didn't see what it was?" Bev asked. "Didn't see anyone around?"

"Not a soul." She wrung her hands nervously. "Thank goodness I'd put the horse in the pasture already. Can't imagine what I'd do if I lost Gus. It's bad enough his barn was destroyed—"

"If you need a place to board him, there's room at the inn stables," Bev said. "Sin won't mind."

Alice gave her a grateful smile. "You're a gem, Bev."

They turned the corner and walked up to the farm. More of the barn littered the ground here, and, at the end of the dirt path, there was...well, it wasn't really a crater, but it certainly looked like *something* had exploded. The ground had been swept away in an almost perfect circle, and while there wasn't a fire, there appeared to be skid marks on the ground.

"Well, I'll be," Earl said, looking at Bev. "Doesn't look to be the same thing that happened to my shop, does it?"

"What happened to your shop?" Alice asked with a frown. "Haven't been to town much this year."

"It burned down the other day." Earl picked up a piece of wood nearby then another. "But this looks to be something else entirely, doesn't it, Bev? Maybe just a coincidence?"

Bev nodded, but she'd learned coincidences didn't happen all that often in Pigsend anymore. "What can you tell me about this morning?"

"Oh, um." Alice rubbed the back of her head. "Well, I put Gus out to pasture early. Fed the goats. Said hi to Bathilda as she was walking her property." She sighed. "Then went back inside to make a spot of lunch. Next thing I know…" She gestured around. "As loud as a cannon, I'd reckon."

"Anything strange in the barn?" Bev asked.

Alice shook her head. "Nope. It was empty. Just hay. I'd mucked the stalls this morning so there weren't even droppings."

"And you didn't see anything after the explosion? Anyone running away?"

"No, I told you. Just me and the goats and the horse." She shook her head. "A real puzzler."

"You said it," Bev said, kneeling to inspect the skid marks on the dirt. Biscuit was sniffing around, more interested than usual. Bev didn't want to talk to him outright in front of Earl or Alice, lest they think her touched in the head for talking to her dog, but he seemed as focused as he'd been with in the jug back at Earl's workshop. Something magical was around.

Bev gave Alice a once-over. Biscuit didn't seem interested in her, just the remnants of her barn. But the laelaps lifted his head, nose twitching as he turned to look behind Bev. She followed his gaze and blinked.

Was that the grannies?

"Hello, dearie!" Janet called, waving happily.

The three were picking up pieces of the barn as they went, already carrying armfuls of splintered wood.

Gladys reached down for another small piece. "We heard there was another incident."

"Oh, good, Earl's already here!" Rita replied. "We're ready to get to work."

"Who...are they?" Alice said, turning to Bev.

"They're guests at the inn," Bev said. "Somewhat handy. Helped Earl get his workshop back together after it burned down."

"They're ancient," Alice said.

"They do good work." Earl shrugged.

Biscuit trotted over to greet the grannies with his tail wagging wildly. They scratched him behind the ears and at the base of the tail, which moved so fast it was hard to see.

"Goodness, what a mess," Janet said, putting her hands on her hips. "Rita, why don't you see about picking up all these splinters? Gladys and I will search for some wood to start framing. Earl? Did you happen to bring any nails?"

Earl jumped. "No, no, I didn't. But I can check with the blacksmith. Cleaned my stash out rebuilding my workshop."

"Hop to it, dearie," Rita said, dropping her armful of splintered wood and waddling over to pick up more. "We've got plenty of daylight to work, and I'm sure this lovely farmer—er… what was your name, love?"

"A-Alice," she stammered.

"Alice needs to get her farm back up and running," Rita finished. "Bev, why don't you take her inside for a nice cup of tea, eh? She looks a bit pale. Might need a pick-me-up."

"Oh, um…" Bev *really* needed to be getting back to the inn. She hadn't even put in her meat order for the day, and it was wearing on. "All right. Come on, Alice. Let's see about that tea."

~

Alice's farmhouse was rather large considering she lived alone, with a well-stocked kitchen and plenty of seating. Alice put on a kettle and joined Bev at the small, circular table, as she shook her head. Biscuit curled up by Bev's feet but seemed awake to listen to the conversation.

"I wish I could tell you I saw something strange, Bev, but it was all normal. No one's been in my yard at all today. Or if they were, they did a good job hiding from me." She stared at the window as the grannies conversed with Earl. "Are you sure they can handle—"

"Quite sure," Bev said. "Earl's seen what they can do up close, and you know how picky he is about his craft."

"Too right." She folded her hands. "He inspected the barn about two weeks ago, too. Wood was holding up against the elements, nails seemed to be in good shape." She met Bev's gaze. "What kind of thing can blow down a whole barn without being seen?"

"I haven't a clue," Bev said. "But I hope it's not the same thing that set Earl's workshop on fire."

"Guess you're back on the job, huh, Bev?" She smiled weakly. "Got another mystery to solve."

"It would appear so." She gazed out the window at the lush trees lining the property in the distance. Back during the sinkhole debacle, Bev had found a magical river underground. The queen's soldiers had installed a deflection device that had effectively stopped the river from flowing into town.

She started. Did *that* have anything to do with the recent explosions?

"Has anyone been around lately?" Bev asked. "Anyone who might be irked at you for some reason? Or anyone who might want to destroy your barn to get back at you for something?"

"Well, maybe Bathilda," Alice said with a chuckle. "One of my goats got onto her land the other day, and you would've thought I was about to steal her mother's pearls."

"Bathilda?" Bev frowned. Alice's neighbor was as friendly as they came—save her desire to get Bev's rosemary bread recipe. She sold her crops at the twice-weekly farmer's market on this side of town. It had been a few months since Bev had seen her, since said market was on hiatus until there were crops in the spring. "Is that recent?"

"Well, I hadn't seen her since before the solstice. Pretty good at keeping my livestock on my own property, but you know how goats can be. Have one who's a little bit of a wizard getting in and out of pens. He was halfway onto Bathilda's property before I found him. She wasn't too happy, waving around her broom and trying to shoo us both off her land. I didn't think much of it." She lifted a shoulder. "Maybe Bathilda just hates goats? She grows nothing but produce on her land, so maybe she was worried he'd get into the early plants."

It was possible. Hadn't Earl said something about Bathilda paying him for something? "I see. Well, if you think of anything, let me know. I'm going to go outside and check on Earl and the grannies."

"Is that what you're calling them?" Alice chuckled. "That's a good name for them. How long are they in town?"

"Oh, who knows?" Bev said. "They're being

awfully dodgy about why they're here."

"Unless they showed up without me knowing, can't say I've ever seen them around these parts before," Alice said. "If that's what you were thinking."

Rita waddled by, grinning at her sister as she carried a large, heavy-looking piece of wood.

"There's something off about them, but I haven't quite figured out what it is yet," Bev said.

"Well, if they can rebuild my barn, I'll be grateful to 'em. My horse is getting on in years. Was all I could do to get a shoe on him yesterday."

Bev nodded as Janet walked by. "If you need a place to house him tonight, the inn stables are open. Just drop him off and I'll make sure he's well taken care of."

"Thanks, Bev."

~

Bev and Biscuit left Alice in her house, joining Earl as he spoke with Gladys about what they needed—which appeared to be framing wood and paneling.

"Usually have more on hand, you know, but most of it got burned up in the shop," he said. "So I need to take a trip to Middleburg."

"Oh, we'd be happy to go," Rita said, walking by with another large piece of wood.

Janet joined her. "Never been to Middleburg."

"How far's the trip?" Gladys asked.

Beasts and Baking

"About an hour, by wagon," Bev said. "I've got one back at the inn you could borrow. And Sin needs a bit of exercise."

Rita cooed. "That lovely mule in your barn?"

"Sweetest thing I've ever seen." Janet nodded.

"Why in the world are you calling her Sin?" Gladys asked.

"She used to have a reputation, so I hear," Bev said.

"Doesn't have one now."

"Took as many carrots as we could feed her."

"Just a sweet thing."

"Well, if you've won Sin over," Bev said, "feel free to use her and my wagon. I'm sure she'd like the trip."

Earl, Gladys, and Janet made plans on where and how they'd meet up, while Bev kept an eye on Biscuit, who was sniffing the ground again.

"Earl, before you go," Bev said, "did you say you were doing something for Bathilda?"

"Eh? Oh, yeah. Nothing in the workshop, though." He nodded toward her farmland in the distance. "She wanted me to build her a pen."

"A pen?" To Bev's knowledge, Bathilda didn't have any livestock. "For what?"

"I'm not really sure," Earl said. "But she wanted it in a hurry. Paid me well for it, too."

"Have you seen her since?"

"Just the once when she came by to drop off

payment," he said. "Why?"

"Might walk over and see if she heard anything," Bev said. "I suppose I'll see you lot for dinner tonight?"

"Of course," he said. "What's on the menu?"

"Oh, it's pork shoulder tonight, dearie," Janet said with a bright smile. "We already popped in to pay the butcher."

"Be a lamb and add some apples, if you have them," Rita said.

"I do love pork and apples," Gladys said with a grin.

"I think I might have a few left over," Bev said. "Pork it is."

Bev hopped the relatively small fence over to Bathilda's yard, and Biscuit followed his nose. Bev scanned the property for the fence Earl had built, but she didn't see any sort of livestock pen. Then again, there was a thicket of trees in the middle of the property, so it could've been beyond that.

"What do I care about a livestock pen?" Bev muttered to herself. "Stay close, Biscuit. Don't run off."

Although they got along well enough, Bev was sure Bathilda wouldn't want a mischievous laelaps mucking about on her property, even if it was still too early to plant anything outside. He wasn't as bad as a goat to her early crops, but she didn't want to chance a bad encounter.

And yet, the moment the words left her mouth, Biscuit seemed to have scented something and took off toward the thicket of trees.

"Biscuit!" Bev called as she dashed after the surprisingly fast small creature. "Biscuit, get back here!"

She'd thought they'd come to an understanding on following directions, but it was clear that understanding only held when there wasn't something more interesting around. Whatever he'd scented, he was *very* keen on it.

"Biscuit!"

He stopped, sniffing what appeared to be a large pile of dung, allowing Bev to finally catch up to him.

"Biscuit, you have to *listen* when you're—"

Something whizzed through the air, barely missing the laelaps and Bev. An arrow landed in the ground nearby, and Bev whirled around as a small figure carrying a crossbow came running up to her.

"Get off my—Oh. It's you, Bev."

Bathilda only came up to Bev's elbow, but she looked fierce enough to take on a person twice her size. She had white hair and leathery skin that had seen many years tilling in the fields. Her sweet smile was gone, and in its place was a scowl that made her almost unrecognizable. She wore thick leather boots and had a leather apron similar to the one Gilda wore in the blacksmith's shop.

She lowered the crossbow, though her misgivings hadn't seemed to disappear completely as she glared at Biscuit, who was circling Bev, sniffing the ground. "What in the world is that thing?"

"It's my…dog," Bev said, deciding not to mention he was a magic-detecting creature. "Sorry. He got loose."

"I see." She sniffed. "Well, if you've got him now…"

"Actually," Bev picked Biscuit up as he was starting to wander again, "I wanted to ask you a few questions."

"Yeah?" Her snarl was back. "About what?"

"Alice's barn, just now." Bev tossed a thumb behind her. "Collapsed."

"Did it now? Perhaps she should've taken better care of it."

Bev laughed, a little nervously. "She said it sounded like a cannon had been fired. You must've heard it."

"Nope." The farmer didn't meet Bev's gaze. "Didn't hear a thing. Can't hear much anymore, you know. Getting old."

"You didn't notice anything out of the ordinary on her property, did you?"

"Nope. Too busy tending to my own business." She twitched her arm like she was eager to use the crossbow, especially as Biscuit's nose pointed toward the thicket again. "Is that all?"

"No. Earl's workshop was destroyed, too. Burned down. Everything inside, gone." Bev waited for a reaction, but all she got was more scrutiny from the farmer.

"What do I care if his place burned down? I wasn't there."

"No, but he said he'd made you a fence, right?"

"Perhaps he did, but it's none of your business."

"Earl asked me to find out who might've been responsible for his place. And with Alice's barn just now—"

"It sounds like we have an epidemic of shoddy craftsmanship in town," she said with an uncharacteristic sneer. "Earl should take better care of how he stores his flammables, and Alice's old barn has been on the brink of falling for years now. Not surprised one big push knocked it over." She adjusted the crossbow in her hands. "Now if that'll be all, please kindly *remove* your dog from my property before I remove him myself."

Bev frowned. Bathilda had never been so short with her. "Well, if you remember—"

"I said *goodbye*, Bev. If I see that dog on this property again, I won't hesitate to shoot him, so I suggest you get a handle on him."

Chapter Nine

"What in the world's gotten into Bathilda?" Bev asked herself as she and Biscuit made their way back to the inn, Gus plodding behind. She set him up in the barn in the stall next to Sin's, which was already empty. Her wagon was gone, too. Gus seemed a bit perturbed from all the excitement of the day, but happily took a carrot and some oats from Bev before settling down.

When Bev walked into the kitchen, the pre-ordered pork was already waiting, along with a note from Ida with an explanation. Bev got to work immediately, as pork shoulder was a cut that needed a lot of low and slow cooking. But with the right sort of spices, and a little vinegar, she could make it fall-off-the-bone tender in the time left until dinner.

She worked quickly, stoking the oven so it would be a little warmer and slicing all the excess fat off the meat. It was beautifully marbled, of course, and she placed it in her large roasting pan with an assortment of herbs—including her rosemary.

"That's right. They wanted apples," Bev muttered to herself. She wasn't sure what she had down in the root cellar, other than a few crates of potatoes and other vegetables, but she ventured into the dark, damp space. She pulled out some of the crates, finding potatoes, yams, potatoes, parsnips, potatoes, turnips, and more potatoes. Then, in a back corner in a small bag, four apples.

"Perfect."

She set one aside in the empty barn for when Sin returned from her trip to Middleburg. The old mule was fed a healthy diet of carrots, so an apple was a rare treat.

Bev quartered the remaining three apples and tossed them into the roasting pan then put the top on and hoisted the whole thing into the oven. It was two in the afternoon now; she'd check it around four to make sure it was falling apart appropriately. Not that the grannies would mind. Bev had a feeling she could serve the meat raw, and they'd gobble it up.

She worked on the rest of dinner, thinking about her curious guests. For having business in town, they certainly didn't mind packing up and heading to Middleburg with Earl. Were they waiting for someone? That seemed the most likely, as they didn't seem to care what they filled their days with, only that they were full.

But who could they be waiting for?

"Come now, Bev, they aren't hurting anyone. Quite the opposite." Bev glanced at Biscuit, who was asleep in front of the hearth.

The laelaps seemed to sense he was being watched and lifted his head. He was still dusty from Bathilda's farm, which got Bev thinking again about the farmer's odd behavior. Surely, Bathilda was just having a hard day. Perhaps her hip was bothering her or something.

And perhaps the pen she'd had Earl build for her was for cows. Maybe she was getting into the business.

Bev paused, glancing at the kitchen door. There was one easy way to find out.

She left the meat cooking in the oven and crossed the street to the Witzels' butchery, but she stopped before she got there. Bardoff and his gaggle of students were standing in the middle of the street, watching something in the air.

"What in the...?" It seemed to be a lantern floating in the sky—and for once, the children actually looked interested.

"You see, children, when the air inside the

lantern gets hot, it sends the whole lantern up into the air," Bardoff explained, nodding to Bev. "Much like we learned with Bev, fire and heat can do many different things."

"We also learned that with Earl's barn," came the snide remark from Grant.

"Yes, that too," Bardoff said, with a roll of his eyes. "Why don't you try your lanterns and see what you get?"

The kids broke off into small groups—Bev's "miscreants" in their own trio—and set to building a lantern like the one currently floating above their heads.

"Certainly seem to have their attention today," Bev said. "But I wonder what benefit knowing how to make a lantern fly has on their adult lives?"

"Pssh. You sound like Etheldra," Bardoff scoffed. "The point of education is to broaden minds. Sometimes you have to take a roundabout way of getting there. If it means teaching them how to set things on fire to teach them about the difference in air pressure, so be it."

"You could, of course, step into the butchery and teach them the parts of a cow," Ida drawled, coming to stand next to Bev. "Flying lanterns, Bardoff? Really?"

The teacher didn't answer because young Tallulah Punter had set her whole lantern on fire.

"He certainly has funny ideas," Ida said.

"He's not the only one," Bev said. "Thanks for the meat, by the way. How much do I owe you?"

"Not a silver. The grannies paid *double* what it was worth." Ida snorted. "No clue where they got all their gold, but they sure have it."

"Indeed, they do," Bev said, filing that tidbit away for later. "Listen, I had somewhat of a random question for you. Have you heard of Bathilda Wormwood getting cows or goats or any kind of livestock?"

"Bathilda? Old Bathilda from out west?" Ida shook her head. "She just grows produce, doesn't she?"

"Thought she did, but Earl built her a fence recently." Bev glanced around at the kids, once again noticing Valta was missing. "Then her neighbor's barn collapsed."

"Who? Herman?"

"Alice," Bev said. "The grannies are already on it. Might have it back up this evening."

"Oh, Bev. You can't suspect someone based on a fence." Ida chuckled.

"It's not the fence, but that she nearly took Biscuit and me out with a crossbow this afternoon," Bev said. "Alice says she's been very unfriendly lately, too. Almost like she's hiding something. Just trying to rule out the obvious answers."

Ida clicked her tongue. "Looks like we've got a full-fledged mystery on our hands, don't we?" She grinned as she moved closer to Bev. "Are you gonna go sleuthing? Sneak onto her property and see what she's hiding?"

"Well, I was hoping to avoid that by you telling me she was selling you beef," Bev said.

"Sorry, friend. Haven't seen Bathilda in weeks." Ida shrugged. "Whatever she's got in those pens, she isn't selling for meat. If she's even selling them at all."

The usual suspects arrived for dinner, including Earl and the grannies. Earl had been flabbergasted when Janet paid for the suite of lumber in Middleburg that had been loaded onto Bev's wagon, and, although he'd said it wasn't necessary, the granny had insisted upon it. Yet again, the question of who these strange women were and how they came into all their gold bounced around in Bev's head, but for now, she was just grateful they were helping get everyone back on their feet.

Once everyone was gone or upstairs for the night after dinner, Bev went to the kitchen to wash dishes and think. Proximity to Alice's barn didn't make someone guilty, and neither did being rude. Bathilda could've just woken up on the wrong side of the bed or had a thing against dogs.

Bev glanced at Biscuit, who was in a dead sleep next to the dying embers of the fire. He was interested in *something* in her yard. She hadn't seen him so animated since he'd found a magical bauble in a pie during the Harvest Festival.

But just because something's magical doesn't mean it's destroying workshops and barns.

Ida was magical, and all she did was chop up meat and spin wild conspiracy theories.

Still, Bev couldn't get the thought out of her head, even as she finished tidying up the kitchen and rearranging the chairs. She ascended the stairs to her room, Biscuit sleepily trotting at her heels, but after she blew out the candle, she lay awake, staring at the ceiling.

"Now, Bev," she said to herself, "don't you be getting any wild hairs. We don't need to be trespassing again."

Biscuit lifted his head in the dark, his ears twitching in the moonlight.

"There's nothing on Bathilda's land that concerns us," Bev said. "Besides that, Bathilda's whatever-she-might-have wasn't anywhere near Earl's shop."

Biscuit let out a low sniff.

"Unless whatever Bathilda's got has made her a target, and someone is trying to threaten her."

Another sniff.

"That could explain the reason for her rudeness," Bev reasoned. "She could've thought we were whoever's threatening her."

A ruff.

Beasts and Baking

"But we really can't be just…gallivanting around at night," Bev said, lifting her head. "I mean, we have the inn, we need to sleep. Besides that, it's just not proper, you know."

Sniff.

"Well, that was different," Bev said. "There were *sinkholes.* One right in front of the inn. Nobody was doing anything about it."

Ruff.

"Bathilda should've just come out with it if she wanted help. She probably doesn't."

Biscuit stood and hopped off the bed, his soft feet padding toward the door.

Bev sighed. "Well, I suppose since you're up… we might as well take a little stroll, eh? Now where did I put that glowing stick…"

~

Bev's glowing stick—a knotty piece of lumber with mushrooms growing on it that illuminated in the dark—was right where she'd left it in the shed, and before she knew it, she and Biscuit were walking down the silent road toward Bathilda's house.

"Just out for a stroll," Bev muttered to herself, looking around for anyone who might be out. "Just a little walk down the street."

The laelaps needed no light, his nose pressed to the ground as he moved quickly along the dirt road. Bev repeated the lie to herself as she drew closer to Bathilda's farmlands. She left the glowing stick along the fence line, hoping the clouds would stay away from the moon to illuminate her way. The white tip of Biscuit's tail caught the scant light, and she was able to follow the laelaps across the barren gardens.

Biscuit ducked under a fence, and Bev recognized Earl's handiwork. This must've been the fence he'd constructed for her. Up ahead, Biscuit let out a low *ruff*, and Bev easily hopped over the fence. Behind her was tall, hardy grass that had survived the winter, but beyond the fence, it seemed to be all gone. Or at least, very low—like it had recently been cut.

"Or eaten," she muttered. "Biscuit? Are you all right?"

She might've been hasty coming out here. There was no telling what Bathilda might be herding in this arena. Sure, it might've been the run-of-the-mill cows or sheep, but Rosie Kelooke had demonic chickens that had left scars on Bev's shins the last time she'd tangled with them.

"Biscuit?" she whispered into the darkness, worrying when she didn't hear the telltale *ruff* from the laelaps. "Biscuit? Come back here." She let out a low whistle. "Biscuit? *Biscuit?*"

She nearly jumped out of her skin when a loud noise echoed through the darkness. She put her hand over her beating heart, taking a shaky breath and listening.

"Baaaaaaa."
"Ruff."

"Goodness," she whispered, shaking herself. "Biscuit, where are you?"

She followed the sound of his low barking until she found him standing in front of…the strangest-looking sheep she'd ever seen in her life. No, it wasn't a sheep—it just had the fluffy wool of a sheep. It had a long, naked black neck, a pointed snout, and beady eyes like a sheep. Four bare legs with hooves like a sheep. But the wool was…

"Purple?" Bev breathed. "Are these…?"

Tanddaes. The name came to her like a distant memory, something her dear friend Merv had told her about. He'd used their wool to make a blanket he'd entered in the Harvest Festival competition. She'd thought he'd dyed it to get that robust color, but clearly, it just came off the creature that way. Even in the dark, it was vibrant and deep.

"Why in the world would Bathilda be testy about breeding these?" Bev wondered until Biscuit began sniffing the wool and salivating—like he was eager to take a piece of it for himself.

"Keep your chompers off," Bev said, using a tone that meant business.

Biscuit retreated, but only a little.

These creatures were *magical*. That, perhaps more than their unique coat, was the reason for the secrecy. The queen had funny ideas about magic and seemed to want any kind she didn't approve of eradicated from the earth. Where these creatures landed, she didn't know, but she had a hunch it was on the side of "not approved."

"I wonder what—"

Voices echoed from up ahead, and a small pinprick of light seemed to be drawing closer. Bev grabbed Biscuit by the midsection and pulled him behind one of the large creatures—as there was nowhere else to hide. She held her breath, peering over the puffy purple wool as Bathilda came hobbling up with a tall, lanky person beside her.

"Damn trouble these things are. Eat everything green they can get their teeth onto," she said. "Never again will I agree to this."

"They're quite healthy." The man had a soft, unctuous voice, like he was used to swindling people. "How many do you have?"

"Twenty-five," she said. "Maybe more. Hard to tell with their thick wool which ones may be pregnant and which are just in need of a haircut."

"Mm." The man approached the closest one and ran his fingers along the wool. "Very nice. This will fetch a great price down in Lower Pigsend."

"I should say so!" She crossed her arms over her chest. "Now when can you take them off my hands? Too many of the queen's soldiers are floating around for me to feel comfortable holding onto them for much longer."

"I'll confer with my boss. How does a thousand gold coins sound?"

Bev had to cover her mouth to keep the gasp of surprise from coming out. A *thousand* gold coins? For twenty-five purple sheep? They must be quite rare.

Based on the way Bathilda was chewing her cheek, the price must've been less than she'd anticipated. "I'll take it, but only if you get them off my land within the next week. Already caused enough problems with my neighbors."

Bev lifted her head. Were these creatures causing all the mayhem? She hadn't a clue what tanddaes did or if they could set a workshop on fire, but it was certainly close enough to Alice's barn to have caused that destruction. Still, before she confronted Bathilda, she needed more information.

And for that, she'd have to visit an old friend.

Chapter Ten

It had been weeks since Bev had seen Merv—and as Bev counted them, she felt positively awful she hadn't been out to visit sooner. Granted, her friend lived in a tunnel some ways out of town, and the sheer amount of snow on the ground had made even walking to the miller difficult. But Merv was a dear, and Bev vowed she'd be out to visit more often.

First, though, she toiled through her morning chores, getting the bread rising, the pots ready for the evening's dinner, and even taking a moment to chat with Allen. She decided to keep all mention of potentially illegal, magical sheep to herself for the moment, at least until she knew more about the creatures. But their conversation was yet again short-lived, as the grannies descended upon the blueberry muffins with gusto.

"Will you be coming with us to Alice's to finish up?" Rita asked Bev, licking her fingers.

"Not today," Bev said. "I've got to visit a good friend out of town. And believe it or not, I should be staying closer to the inn than I am. Never know when someone else might come along looking for a room."

Not to mention Bev's gigantic list of chores that had remained untouched since the kids had helped her deep clean the kitchen. There were still floors to wax and walls to wash and curtains to clean and… This newest mystery couldn't have come at a worse time.

"Well, take it easy, dear," Janet said. "Rest is good for the soul."

"I could say the same to you, but you don't seem to need any, either." Bev chuckled. "I take it Alice's barn will be back up today?"

"We'll be taking her sweet horse back with us," Rita said. "Hopefully, Sin won't be lonely by herself."

"She enjoys her silence," Bev said, before looking down at Biscuit. "And don't you go riling her up either. You stay inside and be good."

"You aren't taking Biscuit with you?" Rita asked.

"Er…" The last time Biscuit had gone to Merv's,

he'd torn up the place. "No. He's going to stay here and guard the inn for me."

Biscuit let out a *ruff* and walked to the fire, lying down and going to sleep.

"Well, he'll guard the hearth for me," Bev said with a chuckle as she picked up her glowing stick. "I should be back midday. Better get on before the morning slips away from me."

"What in the world do you need that for?" Gladys asked, nodding to the stick.

"Oh, um… Merv lives a bit out of the way," Bev said. "Best to be prepared."

~

Bev and the grannies parted ways at the front of the inn. The grannies headed west, Alice's horse clopping behind them, while Bev took a northeast turn at the town square. She passed Trent Scrawl's farm, waving at the curmudgeonly farmer who seemed to be preparing his garden for another year of pumpkins to enter into the Harvest Festival competition. That, or he was keeping a wary eye out for his sometimes-nemesis Herman Monday.

Bev kept walking, crossing over hills and unclaimed land out of town until she found the entrance, which was almost completely overgrown. She pulled at the vines and other winter growth until revealing a large tunnel, big enough for a creature about two feet taller than she was. But she still let the glowing stick illuminate her path, lest she trip over an errant root.

Up ahead, Bev spotted the orange door with green shutters at the end of the tunnel. As she drew closer, more of the same mushrooms that dotted her glowing stick illuminated her path. She stuck the stick in the wall and dusted her hands on her shirt. Regrettably, she was coming empty-handed; perhaps she should've brought a loaf of bread or maybe some tea from Etheldra's shop.

No use worrying about that now. She walked up to the door and rapped three times, standing back and waiting. She hadn't told him she'd be coming—did he even get the post?—and she couldn't be sure he was even home.

A loud rustling sound echoed from the other side of the door and it swung open, revealing a mole even larger than Vellora Witzel. He was covered in black fur, with nearly invisible eyes. The tip of his snout was bright pink, and his nose twitched happily as he took her in.

"Bev!" His long claws tapped together. "My goodness, it's been a while. I thought you'd forgotten about me."

"Never," Bev said, not *actually* sure she could forget someone like Merv. "Just been quite cold and snowy up in Pigsend. Surely, you get a little bit of the chill down here?"

"Oh, I heard all about the snowy winter you've been having. Very glad I live down here!" His whiskers bounced. "Come in, come in, I was just putting on a kettle." He paused, looking beyond her. "You didn't bring that little troublemaker, did you?"

"No." Bev smiled. "Biscuit's back at the inn."

"Then make yourself at home!"

Bev walked into the quaint little abode, taking a moment to appreciate the small changes since the last time she'd been there. The curtains were new, now a white lace, along with the blanket on the couch, which was a vibrant red. Bev scanned the room for signs of the tanddaes wool, but Merv didn't have any out.

"I can't wait to hear *everything* that's gone on since the Harvest Festival," he said, sitting down in the chair opposite Bev.

"Not much has happened over the winter, other than we got a lot of snow," Bev said. "Oh, and the Witzels were blackmailed."

"No!" Merv gasped. "Really? By whom? Because of Ida's magic?"

"Actually, no. Surprisingly, it was quite mundane." Bev didn't know how much Merv knew about the war between queenside and kingside, and he probably didn't know the details about registrars and needing to update service records. "Vellora's wartime record was being held hostage by a perfidious administrator."

"My goodness," he said. "How did you manage

to get them out of that one?"

"That story is too long for the time I've got for this visit," Bev said. "Lots to do back at the inn, unfortunately."

"So this isn't just a social visit?" It was hard to tell from his tiny, black eyes, but he looked excited. "Is there another *mystery* afoot?"

"Well, I can't say I'm not happy to see you," Bev said. "But yes, I had a few questions. Specifically about those creatures called…tanddaes, I think you called them?"

"Don't tell me one's showed up in Pigsend!"

"More than one."

"Oh, please. Spare no detail." He rose and headed into the kitchen. "I'll put on a pot."

"Well, a few nights ago," she began, "Earl, the resident carpenter, his workshop burned down. Now, you know fires happen, but Earl seemed to think something—or someone—was behind it. So he asked me to look into it."

"Naturally," Merv said from the kitchen.

Bev cracked a smile. "He seemed to think a trio of teenagers might be responsible. I talked with them, and, of course they acted guilty, but there wasn't really anything I could do to coax the truth out of them." She smoothed the fabric of the knitted quilt nearby. "I thought, perhaps, someone might've been targeting Earl's workshop to get back at someone he was making furniture for, but that doesn't seem likely now that Alice's barn went down yesterday."

"Another fire?"

"That's the thing," Bev said, leaning forward. "It looked completely different. Like it had been blown down in a nasty storm. And I'd chalk it up to coincidences but—"

"But it seems a bit too related, I agree."

Merv walked out holding a tray with a teapot and two cups. Bev had to school her expression to not gawk at the size of them; the cup was roughly the size of the bowl she used to proof her bread.

"Sugar?" he asked, placing the tray on the table in front of Bev.

"No, thank you." Bev picked up the tea as best she could and took a sip. "Delicious."

"So Alice's barn—is there any connection with Earl's workshop?"

"Not *really*," Bev said. "She didn't see a soul out there. Could've been the kids, but why would they be all the way on the other side of town?"

"You never know what they might be up to," he said with a sniff. "Children are awful. Glad I never had any."

Bev couldn't imagine what a baby Merv might look like and thought better than to ask. "Well, they're not off my list, but they're not at the top of it anymore."

"Anyone new in town?"

"Yes, as a matter of fact." Bev took another ginger sip of the tea, finding she needed both hands and a strong grip to lift it. "A trio of interesting ladies. They're…well, they're old. Quirky. Very sweet—seem to have lots of money, too. Hearty appetites. And they've rebuilt *both* Earl's shop and Alice's barn."

"Hm." Merv sat back. "Do you think they're causing the destruction by accident?"

"I'd say that except they were with me during the first incident," Bev said. "They said they're in town on business but won't say what it is."

"Have you asked them if they know what's going on?"

"Well… no," Bev began slowly. "But somehow, I don't think they'd answer if I asked. They seem to have a way of twisting the conversation. Kind of like Mayor Hendry." Bev paused. "Who had furniture in Earl's workshop and was acting dodgy about it. When I tried to question her, she magicked me and sent me on my way."

"Mayor Hendry has magic?" Earl asked.

Bev nodded. "I think she's an empath or something like it."

"Hm." He picked up a half-finished hat made of bright green yarn and began working on it while keeping his attention on Bev. "That does seem a good sort of magic for a politician. Being able to sway people and bewitch them. No wonder she's stayed in power."

"There was a fellow who stayed at the inn who had a ring with empath powers. Seemed to be similar to what Hendry can do."

"Empaths are rare," Merv said with a nod. "I've only heard of one or two, and that was only a rumor about a kingdom far away. Had a problem with a monster eating them, too, from what I understand."

"Dear me," Bev said. "You don't think we have to worry about that here, do you?"

"Not at all."

"Is there any way I can avoid being taken by her magic?" Bev asked. "It makes questioning her on unpleasant topics quite difficult otherwise."

"You have that laelaps," Merv said. "He's good for helping you keep your head around magic, you know."

"Is he now?"

"Mischievous little devil. But useful. If you ask him to help you, he'll probably do it. Probably do it better if you promise him a slice of bacon."

"Well, I suppose it's worth a try," Bev said. "Do you think Hendry's the cause of all the commotion, though? It doesn't seem to fit with the type of magic she has."

"No, it would be awfully strange, indeed."

Bev nodded. "The only *other* connection between Alice and Earl is Alice's neighbor Bathilda. Earl had just built her a pen, which is curious because she's a produce farmer. Hasn't had any kind of livestock as far as anyone can remember."

"So you snuck out to her property?"

"She *threatened* me when I was chasing after Biscuit," Bev said, her cheeks warming. "So I thought maybe she had some creature that might be causing all the problems. Which led me to—"

"The tanddaes!" Merv exclaimed, downing the rest of the tea. "Are you sure that's what it was?"

"Can't say I've ever seen that sort of creature before," Bev said. "And the purple was…well, it looked like that blanket you made for the Harvest Festival." She took a sip of the tea, with much difficulty. "They were bleating like sheep, too, but they looked… Well, they didn't look like sheep."

"Must've been. That coat is unique—part of what makes the creatures so desirable."

"Bathilda's buyer said he was willing to pay her a *thousand* gold coins," Bev said.

"How many were there?"

"Twenty-five, give or take a few."

"That seems low," Merv said.

"She seemed like she was eager to get rid of them. Maybe the soldiers coming through town made her nervous." Bev chuckled. "Thought she was gonna take Biscuit's head off when she found him on her property."

"I don't blame her. That laelaps is destructive." His whiskers twitched. "Still finding pieces of half-chewed blankets all over the house. And the fur! I thought I shed, but there's golden fur *everywhere*."

Bev knew that all too well. "The buyer said he was taking them to… Lower Pigsend, I think?" She tilted her head. "Is that anywhere near here?"

"Oh yes!" Merv's whiskers twitched. "It's out the front door."

"F—" Bev turned toward the door she'd walked in. "Front door?"

"Oh, dear Bev, that's the *back* door." He laughed as if she were the silly one. "The front door is right there."

Bev turned to where he pointed, and, almost as if water was stilling on a lake, a door appeared. She blinked, turning back toward what she considered the front door, then back to this new one that shimmered a little as she watched it. Either Merv didn't notice or he was used to it, because he didn't say anything about the strangeness.

"I see." Bev nodded slowly. "I suppose it's not frequented by Her Majesty's soldiers?"

"They don't even know it exists," he said. "Lots of the creatures who used to live on the surface moved into town. Magical creatures, you know. A tanddaes wouldn't be thought of twice."

"Bathilda seemed to want the sheep gone. Said they were causing problems for her neighbors," Bev said. "Which is why I wanted to ask… Is there any way they're responsible? They don't breathe fire or anything like that, do they?"

"Fire?" He chuckled. "Not really. They eat grass and grow pretty wool. That's about…well, that's about it for them."

Bev sat back. "Well, that's disappointing."

"Why do you say that?"

"Earl said the way the fire burned in his workshop was too quick to be just wood. He thought there was an accelerant—initially thought it was the spirits he used to dissolve the lacquer he puts on the furniture he makes." Bev drummed her fingers on the cup. "But maybe we are looking at two separate things. Alice's barn hadn't burned down. It was just in pieces, like something had blown it down. And I can't find a connection between Earl and Alice, unless you count Bathilda. They're on opposite sides of town, too."

"Hm." He started a new row on his bright green hat. "Well, I can say definitively the tanddaes aren't capable of *that* kind of destruction. If you're looking for a creature to be the culprit, it wouldn't be them."

"Do you think it's a creature?" Bev asked.

"Well, I can't say I see a reason for an intelligent person to be destroying barns and workshops all over town."

"Any idea what it could be?"

He let out a low thoughtful noise. "Well, the tanddaes themselves are full of magic—as is their wool. It's why it's in such high demand. Was there magic in Earl's workshop?"

"Yes, actually. Mayor Hendry had given him some resin to put on her chairs," Bev said. "When I sniffed it, it seemed to be that same heady magic she has." She snapped her fingers. "Not to mention Alice's barn sits on the magical river that flows under Pigsend."

"Two very magical places." His nails clicked together as he worked another row. "High concentrations of magic tend to attract magical things—both intelligent and otherwise. I think whatever you're looking for has magic of some kind."

"That doesn't really narrow it down much."

He chuckled. "It narrows it down plenty! At least you know you're looking for something *with* magic instead of something *without*." He switched the blanket around and began knitting again. "Simply rule out anyone who doesn't have magic, and your suspect list will be much smaller."

"The kids don't have magic, most likely. I don't think Bathilda does either, though she's certainly surrounded by it." Bev sighed. "Are you sure the tanddaes don't breathe fire or sprout wings or something like that?"

"Not to my knowledge. And my knowledge is quite extensive." He smiled, as best he could with his long snout and pink nose. "Soon enough another piece will emerge, and you'll have more information that might illuminate your culprit better."

"Hopefully not," Bev said. "We don't need any more buildings going down in Pigsend."

"You have to break a few eggs sometimes." He tapped his long nose. "If you do find out more, come visit? I miss our chats." His whiskers twitched. "And I wouldn't say no to another loaf of that award-winning bread of yours, either."

"I'll make a few extra, just for you."

Chapter Eleven

As much as Bev needed another clue to emerge, she hoped it wouldn't come at the expense of another building. So far, no one had gotten hurt in the calamities, and Bev didn't know how long that luck would hold. Still, without more information, Bev was somewhat stymied in her investigation.

She passed through the shops on the outskirts of town, her mind elsewhere until she spotted the telltale blue of Janet's hair inside Bernard Rickshaw's apothecary shop.

"What in the world are they doing in there?" she muttered to herself.

Not that there was anything *wrong* with being in the apothecary. They'd been working hard; perhaps they needed something to ease the aches and pains from their labor. Or perhaps it was completely innocent.

But the grannies remained something of a mystery to Bev, and perhaps this was her chance to find out what, exactly, they were in town for.

They bustled out of the apothecary, chattering to each other with wide smiles and nary a care in the world. Once they were far enough down the road, Bev hurried into Bernard's shop, hoping he would be able to tell her what they'd purchased from him.

Unfortunately, Bev found herself face-to-face with the gaggle of schoolchildren. They filled the space between the apothecary's counter and the front door—the reason the grannies had been standing near the window. Bev herself couldn't get too far inside, having to scoot sideways to close the door. Even though there wasn't much room to move, there seemed to be even fewer kids in attendance than at the butcher's. But the trio of miscreants were there, clumped together as usual.

Bev peered out the window. The grannies had stopped to chat with Rosie Kelooke, who seemed uncharacteristically pleasant with them.

"What's your favorite tincture ingredient?" the schoolteacher asked Bernard.

"Oh, well..." Bernard rubbed the back of his head. "Probably cinnamon, I'd say."

"Cinnamon?" PJ rolled his eyes.

"Are we making pastries?" Valta said, back in attendance.

"Let's not visit the baker, shall we?" Grant said, making a face. "See him too much as it is."

"Children, why don't we *listen*?" Bardoff said with a warning glance. "Why do you like cinnamon so much, Bernard?"

Bev once again craned her neck to watch the street. The grannies were still talking with Rosie.

"Oh, it's quite useful," he said, opening a tin of powder. "Prevents infection, increases blood flow, and can be used to treat pain in the body." He walked over to the candle. "And it does this, too."

He sprinkled the cinnamon over the fire, which caused multicolored sparks as they burned. "This might not look very dangerous," he said. "But get a load of cinnamon powder near an open flame, and you're looking at a huge fireball!" He looked up, his eyes sparkling in hopes the kids would find it as fascinating as he did.

Based on their bored looks, it hadn't worked.

"Ah, well. Excellent description, Bernard," Bardoff said with a nervous grin. "Let's not set any large quantities of cinnamon on fire, shall we? Why don't we work on making our healing tinctures? Come, come, get into groups, please. It appears Bernard has a customer, so let's let him tend to her, shall we?"

The children moved slowly, and Bev waited,

bouncing on her heels for a moment, until Bernard waved her forward.

"Well, Bev?" Bernard's face brightened as he approached the counter. "Don't tell me Sin needs another calming draught."

"No, she's just fine," Bev said, keeping a watchful eye on the grannies out the window. Rosie seemed to be inching toward her house, which meant the grannies would be moving on soon. *What in the world are they up to*? "What did the grannies want?"

"The gr… Oh! Rita, Janet, and Gladys?" He beamed. "Another tincture for heartburn. You know, old age and all."

Heartburn? That seemed…well, likely, she supposed. But disappointingly mundane. "Surprised they weren't at Alice's still," Bev said.

"Told me they'd finished up first thing this morning," Bernard said. "Amazing how fast they can rebuild things, eh? Here they got Earl's workshop back up in a few hours."

Bev nodded, watching them out the window. For as fast as they rebuilt things, they certainly didn't walk very quickly. "What's in a heartburn tincture?"

"Just some peppermint and grain alcohol," he said. "I'd just made a big batch this morning. Been a lot of it in town lately. Bathilda, Apolinary, Rosie Kelooke, even. Probably all that nasty weather we'd had, made everyone a bit tetchy." He leaned in, glancing Bev up and down. "I assume that's why you're looking for one, right?"

"Y-yes, of course," Bev said. "Old age and heartburn."

He hummed happily as he took down the tin from the back wall and pulled out a small vial, handing it to Bev. She popped the cork, sniffing it and finding it to be exactly what Bernard had described—no weird magical aftertaste.

"Take that right before bed, and you should be right as rain," Bernard said. "Anything else I can help you with?"

Bev shook her head, pocketing the vial. "That's all. Appreciate it." She placed a silver on the counter, looking out the window to make sure the grannies were still in sight.

They weren't.

"It's only—"

"Keep the change!"

Bev hurried out the front door, looking left and right down the street. The grannies had last been talking with Rosie Kelooke, and while Bev wasn't the biggest fan of the retired seamstress—or her demonic chickens—curiosity was getting the better of her.

"Excuse me, Rosie!" Bev said, waving at her before the other woman walked into her house. Bev remained on the outside of the small fence, keeping a wary eye on the chickens clucking ominously on the ground below. They looked harmless enough, with white poufs on their heads and multicolored feathers. But Bev knew better than to cross them.

Rosie turned, giving Bev a sneer as she called from her front porch, "What do you want, Bev? More of my tree?"

"Um… No, not today." Bev chuckled nervously as one demonic chicken clucked as it walked by. "Just wanted to ask what you were chatting with the gr…with my inn guests about?"

"I hardly see how that's any of your concern," Rosie said with a look. "Can't a person have a conversation?"

"They sure can," Bev said. "But…" How in the world could she phrase this? "Just curious, I suppose. They've not been very forthcoming about why they're in town and—"

"And you think they're burning down workshops, I take it?" Rosie asked, lifting her nose higher. "Heard you're back on the case, as it were. Suppose there's not much to do at the inn if you're spending your days uncovering every little mystery that happens in town."

Bev forced a smile. "Well, if you don't want to help, then—"

"We were discussing Bernard's heartburn tinctures," she said. "If you *must* be so nosy."

"Really?" Bev asked. "Why?"

"Well, when I was out tending to my birds the other day, they stopped in and complimented me on my mint. Asked if they could have a bit for their heartburn. I told them it wasn't for sale, but directed them toward Bernard's shop and said that he had the best tinctures in town." She paused, lifting her chin higher. "They merely *stopped by* to thank me for my guidance. Nothing nefarious at all."

"Oh." Bernard had mentioned Rosie was getting heartburn medicine as well. "I see."

"Not *everyone* has some horrible secret that you need to expose, Bev," Rosie said. "In fact, I find their company *far* preferable to yours. Even my chickens found them positively delightful."

Bev wasn't sure that was a vote of confidence. "Well, I do apologize for taking up more of your time, Rosie. One last question: do you happen to know where they went? I'd like to catch up with them, if I can."

Or to follow them from afar to find out where they were going.

"Harrumph." Rosie pointed toward town. "They went that way."

~

Bev rushed down the street, looking this way and that until Rita's red hair caught her attention. They were meandering quite slowly, arm in arm, talking up a storm as if they hadn't seen each other in a long time. They weren't headed back to the inn, nor did they seem to be heading anywhere in particular. But everyone in town seemed to know who they were.

What in the world could their "business" be?

They stopped in to see Gilda at the blacksmith's shop, and Bev hid near Earl's rebuilt workshop as she strained her ears to listen. Although the fires in the shop made it hard to hear, the grannies seemed to leave with a bag full of nails—then headed toward Bev in the workshop. Bev scrambled, jumping the fence to hide in the Norrises's yard before they turned the corner.

Earl walked out of his house, waving them down and greeting them in the side yard. "Really, I must pay you for this."

"Don't you worry your little head about it," Janet said, waving him off.

"Where in the world did you bring all this gold from?" Earl asked. "You're practically saints."

Bev had to agree. In fact, she could see a scenario where the grannies destroyed property, rebuilt it, and asked the owners to pay them for their efforts—except the grannies were rebuilding *and* footing the bill. It just didn't make a lick of sense.

Unfortunately, Bev hadn't done a good job of hiding behind the fence, because Gladys stood in front of her, her gray head cocked to the side.

"What in the world are you doing, Bev?" she asked.

"Oh, um." Bev stood, heat rushing to her cheeks. "Just…um…"

"Bev!" Janet said, walking over. "Well, isn't this a lovely coincidence?"

"How was your visit with your friend?" Rita asked.

"L-lovely," Bev said, climbing over the short fence to join her. "Except he didn't quite help me with what I'd gone to ask him about."

"And what was that, dear?" Gladys asked.

"Well, I was hoping he'd help me figure out what's happening in town," Bev replied, watching them intently. "But so far, he's about as stumped as I am."

"Oh, never you mind about that," Rita said, taking one of Bev's arms. "You have enough to worry about."

"And if you don't, then you should enjoy this beautiful spring weather," Janet said, taking Bev's other arm.

"I love this time of year," Gladys said.

"Yes, me too… Except for all the cleaning I have to do back at the inn." Bev needed an excuse to get away from them so she could keep following them. "Which I should probably get back to, so—"

"Oh, cleaning?" Janet gasped.

Beasts and Baking

"I love cleaning." Rita smiled brightly.

Gladys clapped her hands. "Let us help! Please."

Bev had to fight to hide her grimace. She *did* actually need to continue her spring cleaning—and they'd shown themselves adept at most things they'd attempted. But how was she supposed to find out why they were in town if they were helping her clean?

Before she could argue, she found herself being frog-marched back to the inn with Janet on one side and Rita on the other.

"So you finished up at Alice's? You're quick," Bev said, hoping to get a bit more information out of them.

"Barns and workshops are easy," Janet said.

"It's the houses with rooms that take the most time," Rita said.

"We would've spent more time at Earl's, but he was a little too particular about his cabinets," Gladys said.

"Which is his right, cousin," Rita said.

"Indeed."

"Do you just travel the countryside rebuilding structures that fall down?" Bev asked. "Or is this a special trip?"

Janet smiled. "We go where we're needed."

"And where the wind blows," Gladys added.

Rita grinned. "And where the food's good!"

"Needed?" Bev said as she opened the front door

to the inn. "Do you know where you're needed, or are you—"

They didn't answer, setting immediately to tidying everything they could get their wizened hands on. Gladys took down the curtains so she could wash them outside. Rita moved the table and chairs to get to the rug she said she was going to take out to clean. Janet found a rag and was cleaning the hearthstones.

"Are you sure you want to do this?" Bev asked, finally finding her tongue. "Surely, there are other things more important. You said you have business in town to attend to—"

"Oh, not today!" Gladys said.

"You've been such a dear to us," Rita replied, rolling up the rug.

Janet plucked Bev's medal off the hearth and rubbed it with the rag. "Happy to help."

"I have to say," Bev said, a little lost. "You three showed up just in time. Where did you say you were from?"

"Here and there!" Janet chirped.

"What are you in town to do?"

"This and that!" Gladys said, taking the curtains out the front door.

"You just get to baking, dearie. We'll have this spic-and-span in no time," Janet said.

Bev didn't move immediately, torn between asking more questions and actually needing to get to work on the evening's dinner. Eventually, Janet and Gladys's prodding sent her into the kitchen, but she kept the door open to listen to their conversation.

Unfortunately, there wasn't much of one, save the back and forth of them discussing what task to do next. Bev kneaded and shaped her rosemary bread into loaves, chopped vegetables, and got the meat delivery from the butchers in the oven. But there wasn't a discussion of past towns, homes, or anything, just who was going to dust the table and who was going to mop the floor.

The chatter and cleaning continued all the way until dinner, when Earl, Etheldra, and Bardoff joined them. Earl, especially, had grown fond of them, carrying the lion's share of the conversation. But the grannies had a habit of diverting the subject every time he asked about where they'd come from or how they got to know carpentry so well. Based on the suspicious look from Etheldra, she also had her doubts.

When dinner was over, and the locals said their goodbyes, Bev finally gathered her courage to come out and ask them the question that had been on her tongue all day.

"Do you know what's causing all the destruction in town?" Bev asked, putting her hand on her hips. "And are you responsible?"

Janet twittered in laughter. "Oh, goodness, do you think we had something to do with it?"

"We've been here at the inn," Rita said, gesturing to the room.

Gladys nodded brightly. "Just happy to help these lovely townsfolk."

Bev pursed her lips. "You didn't answer my—"

The ground rumbled again, accompanied by a loud roar that reverberated in Bev's bones. The grannies stared at each other, something unspoken between them, before glancing toward the door.

"What in the world was that?" Bev asked.

"I'm sure we'll find out soon enough, dear," Gladys said, adjusting her gray bun, which had gone askew.

Sure enough, loud voices began echoing down the street, calling for help. Gladys, Janet, and Rita put down their cleaning supplies and walked out the door with resignation on their faces. Bev put dinner in the oven and followed suit.

Chapter Twelve

Apolinary's seamstress shop, previously a smart, two-story building with a thatched roof and large front windows, had been reduced to a heap of splintered wood and dust. The moon cast decent light on the wreckage, but it would probably look even worse in the morning. As with Alice's barn, it didn't seem there had been a fire, but rather something large had blown down the entire shop. Or destroyed it from the inside, perhaps.

The grannies had come with Bev and shook their heads wearily.

"Well, my goodness, this is a mess," Rita said.

"Best get to work." Janet picked up pieces of wood nearby.

"Why don't you go check on those poor dears, Bev?" Gladys said, nodding to the group standing near the wreckage. "Make sure no one was hurt."

Bev hurried over, a relieved sigh leaving her chest as she spotted Vicky, her brother, and Apolinary, the former looking quite dusty, but no worse for the wear.

"Are you three all right?" Bev asked. "Goodness, Vicky, you look a mess."

"Just grateful a little dust is the worst of her problem," Apolinary said, plucking a piece of wood from Vicky's hair. "It's a miracle you walked away at all."

"I'm all right," Vicky said, a little shakily.

"What happened?" Bev asked. "We heard this ghastly roar, and... Did that come from here?"

Vicky nodded, her gaze turning to the wreckage of her former place of work. "I'm not entirely sure what happened."

"Start at the beginning," Bev said. "Whatever you remember."

"Well, Apolinary had just left," Vicky said. "I was waiting for my brother to come home, so I stayed downstairs to finish up some pieces for the mayor. The next thing I know..." She gestured to the wreckage. "Grant's pulling me out and looking like I about died."

"You weren't home?" Bev asked the boy.

He shook his head but didn't offer specifics.

"Apolinary?" Bev asked.

"I was at home. Across the street," the seamstress said, nodding to the roof just beyond the fence line. "Heard that noise, then the place collapsing, and I came running. I was absolutely terrified until I saw she was all right." She squeezed Vicky's shoulder again. "Can't imagine what I'd do if something happened to you, Vicky."

"You'd just have a lot more work to do," Vicky replied with a weak smile.

"Psh, work can wait." Apolinary shook her head as she gazed at her former business. "And wait it will. It's gonna take ages to clean this up—let alone find all our fabric. Assuming it's still intact."

"Did you happen to see what caused the collapse?" Bev asked. "Or anything strange?"

"No, my curtains were closed," Apolinary said. "Already in bed. We've been working so hard. I had a headache, so I turned in early."

"Grant?" Bev asked, looking at the younger man. "Did you see anything?"

"Why are you so interested?" he snapped.

"Be nice," Vicky said, glaring at him. "Bev's trying to figure out what's going on. Now why don't you tell her what you heard?"

"Nothing," he said. "I mean, I heard it. But then the house fell. So that was the only thing I was concerned about."

By now, a larger group had begun to gather,

some helping the grannies gather the pieces of the shop. Others came to check on Vicky and offer condolences to Apolinary, whose focus had shifted to her destroyed shop now that it was clear her apprentice wasn't hurt.

"We were already so behind," she said, putting her hand to her head. "Oh, Rosie Kelooke is going to be so mad. She had so many dresses she'd been asking us to finish."

"I'm sure she'll understand," Bev said. "You can't help your shop was destroyed."

"No, but..." She shook her head. "It's a busy season for us. All that fabric..."

"This fabric?" Rita said, walking up with a dust-covered bolt of bright red cloth. "Found a smattering of it."

"That's Rosie's!" Vicky said, standing up and wincing as she grabbed her head. "One of them, at least."

"We'll see about locating the rest," Rita said, inspecting it. "Seems to be a bit dirty, but no worse for the wear."

"W-who are you?" Apolinary asked.

"Rita," she said, nodding to the others, who were picking through the rubble as if they were at the farmers' market. "And that's my sister Janet and our cousin Gladys. We're in town for a bit."

"Suppose it was a good thing we got all that wood for Earl," Janet called.

"Yes, good thing," Bev said. "You might want to grab him so—"

"Already here." Earl walked up to the mess, rolling up his sleeves. "Well, I suppose I was getting a little lazy over the winter without having anything to do. This might take a bit longer than the barn and workshop, you know."

"We're always up for the challenge," Janet said.

"Probably should get an idea of what we need," Gladys said.

Rita nodded. "Make a plan and start first thing."

The four of them huddled among the wreckage as Earl described the seamstress shop as it had been.

"So they're just in town to…fix things?" Apolinary asked, rubbing the back of her head. "Seems oddly convenient for all the things that need fixing lately."

"Indeed," Bev said, turning back to Vicky and Apolinary. "Why don't we let them take over for the moment? I've got extra rooms at the inn. You're welcome to stay until they've got all this sorted. Your brother, too, Vicky."

"My house is fine," Apolinary said. "But Vicky… She lives in the apartment above the shop. Well, lived there." She squeezed her assistant's shoulder. "What do you think? Few nights at the inn? I'm sure I can wrestle up a cup of tea to calm the nerves."

"Got anything stronger?" Vicky asked with a

grimace.

"I'm sure I can find you something." Bev helped her stand. "Come on. Let's get you two settled for the night."

"Room four is available," Bev said, reaching behind the counter to find the key. "You two make yourselves at home. I may have a spare set of pajamas lying around."

"Go on up, Grant," Vicky said. "I want to see about that drink."

Grant hesitated, watching his sister warily, but eventually marched up the stairs with the key and shut the door.

"Poor thing, I think I frightened him," Vicky said. "It's not right, you know."

"What?" Bev asked, walking to the cask of beer and pouring an ale.

"The two of us having to look after one another like this. We should be fighting like cats and dogs, not...well, not trying to parent each other." She wearily settled at one of the tables and gratefully took the ale. "Thank you. I—Oh. Goodness. Hello there, Biscuit."

The laelaps had been roused from his sleep and put his two paws onto Vicky's thighs before resting his head. She scratched behind his ears absentmindedly.

"Come to check on me, eh?" she said softly.

Bev couldn't help but notice how Biscuit's nose twitched, like he'd scented magic on her.

"What a night," Vicky said, taking a long sip of the beer.

"So you don't remember anything at all?" Bev asked.

She shook her head. "I remember sitting at my desk working. Rosie had dropped off a load of fabrics to be made into dresses, and she wanted them back quickly. We already had a large backlog, what with everyone getting into their spring clothes and finding them full of holes from last year."

"Is that normal?"

Vicky nodded. "So I told Apolinary I'd stay behind and get some work done. Next thing I know, Grant's standing over me, pulling me out of the rubble and looking like I'd almost died." She shuddered, clasping the tankard with both hands. "Based on the wreckage, I think I almost did."

"Was there anything funny happening before? Did you see anyone?" Bev asked. "What about Grant? Where was he?" She hesitated. "He sounded a little…guilty?"

"Probably because he was doing something he wasn't supposed to," Vicky said. "I told him he wasn't allowed to hang out with the Climber and Norris kids anymore, but he doesn't listen to me, so he was probably with them." She licked her lips. "I know you probably suspect him, but—"

"I don't think he'd hurt his own sister," Bev said. "Whatever's going on... It's something beyond the normal in Pigsend."

"The normal seems to be chaos, though," Vicky replied. "Especially the last few days. Nobody's house is safe."

"Suppose not." She rose. "You drink that up and have more if you like. Whatever you need to calm your nerves. I'm sure you know this, but Allen brings pastries by in the morning, so—"

At the mention of Allen, her cheeks turned pink.

"What is it?" Bev asked.

"Oh, he's just... Well, he's been cagey again," she said. "Keeping secrets. Honestly, I thought we'd be spending the evening together, but he told me he was busy. Shouldn't have even *been* in the shop when it collapsed." She sniffed, taking another sip. "You think he's heard that I'm here? I'm sure the commotion woke him up. Surprised he hasn't come bursting through the door yet." She looked toward the entrance with an expectant look, as if saying the words would summon him.

"He's a heavy sleeper, perhaps," Bev said, hoping that was true. "He's been nothing but complimentary about you, Vicky. He cares very much about you."

"Does he?" She sniffed. "He always says I'm making a big deal out of nothing. But I don't know.

I keep getting this feeling like…" She sighed. "I don't know if he's leading me on. If he is, I'd just like him to come out and tell me so I can move on."

"Allen's a good boy. Man. Whatever," Bev said. "But if you want, I can have a word with him about it. I'm sure there's a good explanation for whatever's going on with him. There always is."

"Maybe." Vicky finished the rest of her ale. "I should get some rest. Not as if I've got work to do in the morning. But…" She sighed. "Rosie's going to be furious. She wanted those dresses by the end of the week."

"I'm sure she'll understand," Bev said, though knowing the other woman, she might have a few choice words to say about it. "Get some rest. We'll see what things look like in the morning."

Things didn't look that much better in the light of day. Allen had dropped off pastries and left before Bev could even tell him Vicky was staying there. Not that it mattered, because Grant came downstairs to tell Bev his sister wasn't feeling up to leaving her bed today.

"Is she all right?" Bev asked. "Should I fetch the doctor?"

"No, I think it's less her head and more something else." He glanced at the pastries and scoffed, not taking one. "She'll be fine."

"Allen didn't come up to see you guys, did he?"

Bev asked, a little hopefully.

"That chump?" He scowled. "No. He didn't. And I'll thank you not to remind my sister of that. She's already upset enough as it is."

"What about you?" Bev tilted her head. "Are you all right?"

"Just a house," he said with a sniff. "I gotta get to school."

"Where are you going today?" Bev asked. "I assume Bardoff has another riveting lesson planned?"

Grant didn't answer, just walking out the door and slamming it behind him.

"Well, dear boy, if you're trying to allay suspicion, you're going about it the wrong way," Bev said, looking down at the interested Biscuit. "What do you think, Biscuit?"

He sniffed loudly.

After finishing her chores, Bev decided to bring the laelaps to the seamstress's shop. So far, he'd been able to scent out something magical at each of the wreckages. She was hoping he might pick up a trail they could follow or uncover *something* that could shed light on these mysterious happenings.

Apolinary was already there, as were the grannies, who'd left bright and early to get started. The seamstress was describing the way the shop had been set up before to Rita, who was nodding. Her cousin and sister had nearly finished gathering all the large pieces onto Earl's wagon, an astonishing feat, considering the amount that was there the night before. On a smaller cart were piles of dusty fabrics that seemed to catch Biscuit's attention.

"Morning, Bev," Apolinary said as Rita walked away. "How's Vicky?"

"Fine, I guess. She didn't come down this morning." To the seamstress's concerned expression, Bev added, "I did see her brother, who promised me she seemed fine. Just tired. Wanted a day to recuperate."

"We've certainly been burning the candle at both ends," Apolinary said. "To be honest, I wish I was back in bed, too. But if we don't find Rosie's fabric under all this, I'm afraid she's going to have my head."

Bev nodded to the wagon. "Surely, that's the lot of it, right?"

"Missing one or two bolts," she said. "But I'm sure they're around here somewhere. Planning on dropping these off with Vicky later after I give them a good scrubbing—if she's up for it." Apolinary rubbed the back of her head. "I wouldn't press, of course. Happy to let her take the time if she needs it. But between Rosie and Bathilda—"

"Bathilda?" Bev said, quirking a brow. "What's she got you doing?"

"Oh, the usual. Spring's come and people need new clothing. We've had twenty orders for new tunics in the last two weeks alone."

Biscuit was on his hind legs, sniffing the fabrics with his tail wagging.

"What kind of fabric did she give you?" Bev asked. "Was it purple?"

"Purple? No, can't say it was. Vibrant black color. Bit fancy for a farmer, but maybe she's got somewhere nice to be. And—"

It happened in a flash. Biscuit found something delicious and latched onto it with his teeth, pulling the whole bolt of fabric down off the wagon. Apolinary yelped in concern, and she and Bev ran to the laelaps.

"Biscuit, *drop it!*" Bev cried. "Drop it right this instant!"

The dog opened his mouth and released the black fabric. He took a step backward, his tongue running across the top of his mouth as if he'd tasted something bad. Bev knelt to pick up the fabric he'd taken and was relieved to see it hadn't torn.

"Thank goodness," Apolinary said. "What's gotten into your dog, Bev?"

Magic. "Is that Bathilda's?" Bev asked.

"Yes," Apolinary said, inspecting it closer. "Looks to be all right, though." She put the fabric back on the cart, and Bev helped her reload the rest. "I've got to take all these down to the creek to wash the dust off them anyway."

"Why don't I help?" Bev asked, eager to spend

more time with this fabric Biscuit was so keen on—and perhaps find out more about what Apolinary was making for Bathilda. "But instead of going to the creek, why don't we head back to the inn? I've got a setup for washing sheets. We'll have this cleaned up in no time."

"I don't know..." Apolinary said, eyeing Biscuit.

"Biscuit will leave them alone," Bev said with a warning tone to the laelaps. "Or he won't get any beef stew for dinner tonight."

His head wilted.

"He sure does listen well," Apolinary said.

"When he wants to." Bev brightened. "You can check on Vicky, too. I'm sure she'd like to see a friendly face."

"Maybe I could coax her out of bed," Apolinary said with a wistful smile. "We do have an *awful* lot of work to do."

Chapter Thirteen

Bev helped Apolinary bring the stack of cloth around the back of the inn, near the hand pump and water basin. The seamstress ducked inside to check on her assistant while Bev got out the lye and extra basins from the barn. Biscuit lay down near the front door, his golden eyes watching her as she unfolded the fabric.

"What d'ya reckon?" Bev asked, picking up the one he'd seized. "Magical?"

He sniffed, his nose twitching.

"Well, it's certainly not bacon," Bev said, running her fingers along the wool-like fabric. It certainly *felt* like tanddaes. If Bathilda was so concerned about keeping her magical sheep under wraps, why would she send it to be turned into a tunic?

Then again, it was dyed so intensely Bev couldn't see a bit of purple in the fabric at all.

"Vicky's not feeling up to helping," Apolinary said, walking out of the inn. "Says her head's killing her."

"You think we should fetch the doctor?" Bev asked, pumping water into the basin. "She seemed well enough last night."

"She looked like she'd been crying all morning," Apolinary said. "Do you know anything about that?"

Bev nodded, a little sadly. "I think she and Allen are on the outs again. He didn't even stop in to chat this morning, and he hasn't been up to see her at all. Not really something one does to one's girlfriend, is it?"

Apolinary rolled her eyes. "Those two, I swear. They're on. They're off. He's done something to offend her. She's taken something out of context. Back and forth." She snorted. "They just need to get married and get it over with."

Bev smiled. "Would be nice to have another wedding in town. I think the Witzels were the last ones to get hitched."

"Just be nice for them to be out with how they feel about each other," Apolinary said. "You know, I like Vicky. Was glad to take her under my wing when her folks died. I think she's got some funny ideas about the nature of things, but she's a hard worker."

Bev nodded. Vicky had been known to have an obsession with the land and the trees and how they all interacted with one another. She'd thrown a fit when the farmers had suggested rerouting Pigsend Creek, saying it would disrupt the delicate balance of nature.

"Those funny ideas," Bev began slowly. "They don't... I mean, she just has ideas, right? She's not... Well, you don't think she's got any sort of magic, do you?"

"Vicky? Magic?" Apolinary laughed. "Not unless you count the magical ability to take things way too personally."

Bev half-smiled. "Suppose not."

"Then again, Allen *has* been somewhat dodgy of late, so perhaps I can't blame her." She dunked the fabric into the water. "Acting all nervous when he sees her like they haven't been together for years. Won't even come into the shop half the time anymore."

"Hm." Bev took the sopping wet fabric and hung it on the line. "Well, next time I see Allen, I'll be sure to get a straight answer out of him. It's not right he hasn't even come to check on Vicky."

"No, it isn't. But what can you do? The heart wants what it wants," Apolinary said, taking the next sheet into the basin with a sigh. "I don't have enough energy to think about their torrid love affair either. I think Rosie Kelooke is trying to prove I'm ruining the business she'd built in this town. That's why she set us an impossible task. Twenty dresses in a week! And in our busy season, too." She snorted. "I'd half-believe she was responsible for the collapse. Maybe those demonic chickens can grow into the size of a house."

"Maybe," Bev said, not wanting to even entertain that thought.

"I can't even think about what's happening at the shop right now. Earl said they could get it back up in a few days, but… Is that even possible?"

"The grannies seem to think so," Bev said. "And for all their quirks, they do know how to rebuild a structure or two."

"Well, thank goodness for them." She gave Bev a bashful look. "They aren't doing this, right? After all, they're the only thing *new* in town, right?"

"You would think," Bev said. "I've all but ruled them out, though. They were with me when the shop collapsed last night." She turned to Apolinary. "You don't remember anything amiss about yesterday? Anyone strange come to call?"

Apolinary let the fabric drip against the scrub board. "Honestly, Bev, there wasn't a thing strange about yesterday. Not a cloud in the sky, so it couldn't have been a storm. Vicky was all alone, and there was nothing inside the shop that could've caused that sort of destruction." She met Bev's gaze. "Surely, you have some theories about what's going on?"

"A few," Bev said. "The problem is, I can't seem to see a pattern between the three incidents. Earl's was a fire, yours and Alice's were a complete knockdown. Yours and Earl's are in town, Alice's is pretty far out. The only common thread is nobody's seen anything."

"That's the only common thread?" Apolinary asked, hanging the fabric on the line to dry and grabbing another—the black cloth Biscuit had been so keen on.

"Well, there is one thread, but it's not a very good one," Bev said, nodding to the cloth. "Earl had recently built a pen for Bathilda, Alice is Bathilda's neighbor, and you've got Bathilda's fabric right there."

Apolinary started, looking at the fabric before letting out a snort and plunging it into the sudsy water. "You really *don't* have much right now, do you?"

"Not much at all," Bev said. She didn't want to mention Bathilda's magical sheep. "Still, might be helpful if I knew what you were making with that fabric?"

"Just a simple tunic," Apolinary said. "I—" Her eyes bulged as she lifted the fabric out of the water.

The black had leached from the fabric and colored the water, leaving behind a vibrant purple. *Tanddaes wool.* "Oh, no… No, no, no! It was dyed! Bathilda didn't mention that at all." She frantically pulled the fabric from the wash basin, but it was too late. The water had turned black.

No wonder Biscuit was so interested. "I'm sure Bathilda will understand."

"What kind of fabric is this?" Apolinary asked, holding it up. "And what sort of creature has purple wool?" She hung it on the line. "Beautiful color. Why would you want to dye this black, anyway?"

"Haven't a clue," Bev said lightly, though she was sure it was something about avoiding suspicion.

"I probably should head over to her house and tell her," Apolinary said with a defeated look. "Bad enough her clothing delivery is delayed. Now I have to tell her I ruined her pretty fabric." She rubbed the back of her head. "I mean, I think I ruined it. Not sure, actually."

"Why don't I run out there for you?" Bev said, sensing the opportunity. "I'm all caught up on chores here, and you need to get the rest of these fabrics washed and on the line so you can get back to work."

"Oh, Bev, would you, please?" Apolinary said with a grateful smile. "You're such a doll. Thank you."

~

Strictly speaking, Bev didn't want to come right out and accuse Bathilda of having something to hide. She didn't believe Bathilda was directly involved in any of the collapses, but there was *something* fishy about what she was doing. And unless Bev pulled on the thread completely, she'd find herself without any leads at all. There was, of course, Mayor Hendry, who'd had property at Earl's and Apolinary's. And Grant Hamblin, who'd been near Earl's shop and seemed cagey about last night's incident. But Bev could place neither at Alice's.

Nor could she figure out *what* was happening. One fireball, two fireless implosions, and nobody had seen anything at all.

And that *roar* had been otherworldly. Surely, a creature capable of such a sound couldn't be missed.

As she walked down the dirt path toward Bathilda's house, Bev idly wondered if Apolinary had been on to something with her quip about the demonic chickens growing to the size of the house. She didn't think it was a chicken, per se, but if there was a small magical creature—something like a mouse, perhaps—that could've caused all this chaos, it might be a very easy explanation. She made a note to check her encyclopedia of magical creatures when she got back to the inn.

Since Bathilda had come at her with a crossbow the last time they'd spoken, Bev left Biscuit at home. She also made sure to walk down the main path to

Beasts and Baking

the house, avoiding any path that might take her closer to the tanddaes pen. But Bathilda had them pretty well shielded in the thicket of trees, so Bev hoped she was safe there.

She walked up to the front door and rapped three times, stepping back and waiting. After a moment, the door opened, revealing a disgruntled-looking Bathilda wearing an apron and muddy shoes.

"Whatddya want?" Bathilda grumbled.

"Apolinary sent me," Bev said. "You had some fabric you'd sent her to make some clothes?"

The door opened wider. "What's wrong with it?"

Bev cleared her throat, looking around for any sort of weapon. "Don't know if you heard the ruckus all the way out here, but last night, the seamstress's shop collapsed. Same thing as Alice's barn, it looks like."

"And?" Bathilda narrowed her gaze. "I hope you aren't suspecting me of having anything to do with it."

"Not at the moment, no. But your cloth was inside and—"

Bathilda's face darkened even more. "That stuff is pretty expensive. I hope she didn't just toss it."

"No, she found it, and was giving it a rinse to clear the dust off. Unfortunately, whatever you'd dyed it with…" Bev lifted a shoulder. "Seems to have come right off. Nothing left but a pretty purple wool."

"Well, that's all right, then," Bathilda said. "The purple is a dye, obviously. No creature exists with purple wool like that."

Bev forced a smile. "I've heard of one. A tanddae. Like a sheep."

"Yeah?" Bathilda inched backward, as if going to reach for something. "I also hear those are highly illegal. Queen had them wiped off the face of the map."

"Did she now?" Bev gave an innocent look. "Why? From what I know, they're just simple creatures. Like to eat grass."

"Yeah, well, they do more than that," Bathilda said. "Their wool is chock full of magic. Lots of folks want to get their hands on that, you know? Pay a nice sum for it." She shifted. "Not that I know anything about that. I'm just a vegetable farmer."

Bev quirked a brow. "Really?"

"Really."

They stared at each other for a long moment before Bathilda broke her stare, letting out a loud snort. "Well, I suppose it was bound to come out sooner or later." She opened her door wider. "Very well, come on in."

Bev hesitated as she followed the farmer inside, still keeping a wary eye out for any weapons. But she just went to the kitchen and put a kettle on her fire.

Beasts and Baking

"Fancy a slice of acorn bread?" Bathilda asked, grabbing a small brown loaf from her pantry.

"Please and thank you," Bev said, following her to sit at the kitchen table. "I do hope you aren't cross with me for figuring it out. I promise, I'm not in the business of telling anyone's secrets."

The farmer scowled and shook her head as she plated two slices. "Bah. Big mistake is what they are."

"How did you come to have them?" Bev asked, taking the plate from her.

"You know I love the farm," she said. "But I'm getting old. Vegetable farming is wearing on me. My dear cousin from Sheepsburg said I'd do well with them. Told me all they do is eat the grass and grow wool that's highly valuable. And it is, to be sure." She looked around. "Got enough to take a holiday to the south if I wanted."

"But…?"

"But as I said, they're illegal. My cousin told me not to worry, we were so far out in the country, nobody would notice or care." She harrumphed. "That was before all the queen's soldiers began showing up in town." She glanced around as if Dag Flanigan would jump out of the bushes at any moment. "You haven't seen any recently, have you?"

"Not since the solstice. And if I did, I'd steer them away from your farm." She took a bite of the acorn bread. "Delicious, by the way."

"Thank you," Bathilda said. "To both sentiments. Can't tell you how much my stomach's turned over thinking about what might happen if the wrong person happened on my farm."

"Explains the heartburn tinctures," Bev said. To Bathilda's suspicious look, Bev added, "Bernard said you'd been in to get some recently. Said a lot of folks had."

"Seems you've been busy," Bathilda said.

"Just trying to figure out what's going on," Bev said. "Vicky wasn't hurt last night, but if buildings keep collapsing, someone might not be so lucky."

"Yes, thank goodness for that," Bathilda said. "I wish I could help, but my magical beasts have been in their pen this whole time. I keep a close eye on them, you know. The last thing I need is one of them wandering off and getting me into trouble."

"Understandable."

"Hopefully, these things will be out of my hands in the next few days. Found a buyer who'll take them all. Not making much of a profit off them, so I sheared a few of them and wove them into some fabric." She tilted her head. "Hendry was by here a few days ago, asking about them. Haven't a *clue* how she found out, but that's the mayor for you."

"Hendry was here?" Bev said, glancing toward Alice's property. "How long ago?"

"Well, the same day the barn collapsed," Bathilda said. "Sorry for running you off like that.

Too many people sniffing around my property for my liking."

Bev tapped her finger on the table, thinking. "Well, that certainly changes things. What was she here for?"

"She paid me twenty gold coins for a bolt of tanddaes fabric," she said. "Asked me to send it over to Apolinary to make a tunic. Wanted it dyed black. I told her it wouldn't take, but she insisted. That wool doesn't really like to be covered up." She nodded at Bev. "Which is why you're here, eh? Got washed, all the dye came out. The mayor might have a problem with that, but that'll be her problem."

Bev nodded, thinking to herself. Hendry had been seen or had something of hers at or near all three incidents. If that wasn't a pattern, Bev didn't know what was.

Was Mayor Hendry somehow the one destroying property? And if so, for what reason?

"You said the wool enhances magical abilities, right?" Bev asked.

"Aye." She tilted her head. "Not sure the mayor wanted it for that, though. It's pretty indestructible stuff. Keeps out the chill and heat. Just a solid sort of wool. It's not as if Hendry's got any magic to enhance."

Doesn't she, though?

Bev had never outright asked her about her uncanny ability to quiet a room or sway people to her side on an issue. And the last time she'd had an unpleasant conversation with the mayor, she'd ended up halfway back to the inn before she knew what she was doing. If she was going to confront Hendry, she needed to be prepared.

"You didn't happen to see anything else the day Alice's barn collapsed, did you?" Bev asked. "Or anyone else?"

"Can't say I did," Bathilda said. "But if I think of anything, I'll be sure to let you know."

Chapter Fourteen

"Oh, thank goodness," Apolinary said with a relieved sigh. "Bathilda said it was all right?"

"Just make the tunic as is, and that'll be fine."

"I'll be sure to put it in the queue, right after I finish these dresses for Rosie," she said, turning back to the fabric spread over one of Bev's three tables. Apolinary had certainly taken "make yourself at home" to heart, having commandeered another table to hold several stacks of multi-colored fabric. She'd recovered her wire models from the shop, too (although some of them looked a little dented), all wearing nearly-complete dresses in a pretty floral print with pins sticking out of the hems. The floor was covered in scraps and pieces of thread.

Apolinary seemed to notice Bev's gaze and smiled sheepishly. "I really appreciate you allowing me to work here. The grannies say the shop will be back up in no time, but Rosie's really breathing down my neck."

"It's perfectly fine," Bev said, forcing a smile. "There probably won't be a large crowd for dinner tonight. Just the grannies, Etheldra, Earl, Bardoff, and most likely, Vicky and Grant." Bev tipped her head. "And you, of course, if you'd like to stay."

"You've been so kind already," Apolinary said. "But...will there be rosemary bread?"

"Got it proofing right now."

"Then, yes, of course." She glanced at the stairs worriedly. "I do hope Vicky will come down. She looked downright awful earlier when I saw her. I sent her right back to bed."

"Has Allen been by yet?" Bev asked, walking to the window and peering at the bakery across the street. Allen wasn't visible in the front window, but that didn't mean he wasn't hard at work in the back.

"No. The scoundrel." She angrily stabbed the fabric with the sewing needle. "I've half a mind to march over there and kick him in the rolling pin, if you get my meaning."

Bev did and was more than a little annoyed at Allen as she set about finishing up for dinner. How could he be so cruel? Surely, by now, he'd heard about the collapse. Surely, even if he was on the outs with Vicky, he would at least be concerned enough to check on her? She hadn't misunderstood him so greatly, had she?

As she put the bread in the oven, she stared out the window, wrenching her thoughts away from Allen and Vicky and back to what Bathilda had told her. Mayor Hendry *had* been near Alice's barn on the day it had collapsed. Whether that made her guilty was another story, but it certainly explained why she'd been so keen to blame the kids the last time Bev had gone to see her.

With dinner baking, Bev headed upstairs to her room, Biscuit trotting at her feet. She pulled up the loose floorboard to find her stash of extra gold along with a book that wasn't strictly legal. The Encyclopedia of Magical Creatures had come in handy in the past to help Bev look up everything from laelaps to gnomes.

Today, she flipped through the pages until she found the creature she was looking for.

EMPATHS

An empath is a magical being with the ability to feel what others feel. Some empaths have the ability to suggest alternate feelings

> **or attitudes. For this reason, empaths should be treated with extreme caution.**

Not a great amount of information, to be sure. No more than Merv had told her—although her dear moleman friend had indicated Biscuit might be able to help Bev avoid the pull of her magic.

Bev glanced at the clock. She wouldn't have time to confront the mayor today.

"In the morning, then," Bev said to Biscuit.

~

It was a lively dinner. Apolinary (who'd swept up the scrap fabric on the floor) stayed for the meal, joined by the grannies and Earl—who seemed to think they'd be finishing up with the seamstress's shop in another day or two—Bardoff, and Grant. Vicky even made an appearance, sitting meekly next to her brother and picking at her meal.

The grannies spoke animatedly about how lovely the seamstress shop was going to be when they were done and sang Bev's praises about the meal, the inn, and anything else they could think of.

"Just the perfect seasonings in this stew, Bev," Rita said, handing Bev her empty bowl.

Apolinary followed suit. "You're a wizard at that rosemary bread!"

"Hardly," Bev said, nodding to the ribbon above the mantel. "If I was, I wouldn't have earned that ribbon. No magic allowed at the Harvest Festival."

Gladys and Janet laughed as they walked up the stairs. Rita paused to survey the Hamblin siblings. Grant was pushing his plate toward his sister, who was shaking her head sadly.

"Is she all right?" Rita asked.

"Broken heart more than broken head," Bev said.

"Oh, those can be quite difficult, indeed," Rita said. "We'll see about getting her up and at 'em tomorrow. Fresh air is good for the soul."

"Indeed." Bev nodded. "Will the seamstress shop be back up soon?"

"As soon as we can. Bit more complex than a workshop or barn, you know. And we may need to borrow Sin again to get some more wood." She chuckled. "Thought we'd had the lot of it, but your town keeps surprising us!"

"And you've no idea what could be causing all these…surprises?" Bev asked, tempted to ask if they'd seen Mayor Hendry skulking about.

"Oh, I'm sure the culprit will come to light eventually," Rita said. "Or not. If we're lucky, the chaos will just stop!" She beamed. "Have a good night, Bev."

Bev sighed. "Good night, Rita."

As soon as they were upstairs, Vicky pushed away her half-eaten plate and followed, not saying a word to Bev or anyone else. Grant quickly devoured the rest of her food and brought both plates to Bev.

"Let me know if I can do anything for you," Bev said.

"Just keep that baker out of here," Grant said. "Vicky's decided she's done with him. And she should be. Hasn't been by to see her at all. What a louse."

Bev let out a noncommittal sound, and Grant hoofed it up the stairs past his sister.

Bardoff was the next to rise, handing his plate to Bev. "I feel bad for the two of them. They've been through a lot already."

"The grannies said they'll have the shop back up soon. And Grant seems…" She wasn't sure how to phrase it.

"He's got a good heart, deep down. He cares about people very much. But he won't admit to it."

"I know the type," Bev said.

"You know, I was worried when the shop collapsed. He hadn't been at school that day, and I feared the worst. Perhaps a good thing he was out and about."

"He wasn't at school?" Bev frowned. "That's not what Vicky said. Do you know where he was?"

"I assume he was with his friends," Bardoff said. "I'd say something to their parents, but I worry if they find out their children are skipping, they might pull them completely and send them to work. They're all bright children. They could have a stellar future. But right now…" He sighed. "It's just hard to get through to them."

"You're doing great," Bev said. "I'm sure they're absorbing more than you think."

"Thanks, Bev." He smiled and nodded. "Have a good night."

In the morning, Bev rose and did her chores, but her mind was elsewhere. She'd never once *tried* to fight Hendry's special brand of magic. And Bev couldn't even be sure the mayor *was* an empath and not something else.

But unless she found out what in the world was happening in town, Vicky wouldn't be the last person to suffer for it. And the next victim might not be as lucky.

"Okay, Biscuit, listen up," Bev said as they walked toward the town hall. "Mayor Hendry is going to try to magic me into leaving. It's your job to make sure I don't, got it?"

He sniffed, his tail bobbing as he walked beside her.

"I'm not sure *what* you can do, but Merv thought you'd be able to help, so…" Bev exhaled loudly as they came to the front steps of the town hall.

The mayor was in her office, reviewing paperwork. There was a single crease between her eyebrows, the only imperfection on her face. Her lips were the same blood-red color as the cloth Apolinary had been working on for Rosie.

"What can I do for you, Bev?" Hendry said, not taking her focus from the papers. "I'm quite busy at the moment."

"Wanted to ask you about these building collapses," Bev said. "I assume you heard about Apolinary's shop?"

"Ghastly what happened. Vicky all right?"

"Yes…" Bev decided against mentioning Allen. "Seems to be doing fine."

"Well, thank goodness for that." She picked up another paper to read. "Anything else I can help you with?"

"I wanted to ask where you were when the shop collapsed," Bev said, standing awkwardly as there still wasn't a place to sit.

"At home, I believe. It was quite late. I don't like burning the midnight oil, so to speak." A pause. "Is that all?"

Bev decided to just come right out with it. "It's come to my attention that you were at Bathilda Wormwood's house the day Alice's barn collapsed."

Hendry didn't lift her gaze. "Yes, it had already collapsed by the time I arrived. Those lovely guests of yours were hard at work getting it back up."

"And that Bathilda had asked Apolinary to make a tunic out of magical wool—something Vicky was working on when her shop was destroyed," Bev continued. "Not to mention those chairs—"

"Oh, for goodness' sake, Bev, don't tell me you're still thinking *I* had something to do with it?" Hendry sat back in her chair. "That's preposterous."

"I'm just saying you're a common thread," Bev said. "Or…your magic is."

She snorted, and Bev felt a little fuzzy. But Biscuit was quick, pressing his cold nose against Bev's hand and keeping her from being swept away.

"Oh. The dog is back." Hendry glared at him. "I told you I'm allergic."

"Are you?" Bev glared at her. "Or are you just worried he's going to keep you from bewitching me?"

"Bewitching?" She shook her head as she picked up another piece of paper. "You really are grasping, aren't you?"

The fuzzy feeling increased, but Biscuit fought it with a lick to Bev's hand. "Tell me this, then: How did you find out about the tanddaes?"

"What's that?" To her credit, Hendry barely showed any sign of lying.

"The wool you purchased from Bathilda," Bev pressed, "belongs to a creature called a tanddaes. Magical sheep." She folded her arms across her chest. "Bathilda has a flock of them. That's why you were at her house the day of Alice's barn collapse. So you could pick up the fabric and give it to Apolinary."

"Point of fact: Bathilda gave it to Apolinary." Hendry tilted her head. "And I already told you, the barn had long since collapsed by the time I got there."

The magical feeling was almost overwhelming now, along with the strong urge to stand and walk out of the office.

Biscuit growled then let out a low bark, and the spell broke.

"Jo." She glared at her. "Stop it. You're not making yourself look innocent here."

"Oh, balderdash," Hendry muttered. "Fine. Yes. I have magic. Not a lot, mind you, but enough to be getting on with. Certainly enough that should the *wrong* person come asking about it, I'd find myself on the business end of a pair of handcuffs, so I'd appreciate it if you'd keep that fact to yourself."

"I wouldn't dream of telling," Bev said. "But be honest with me: What in the world is going on?"

"With the buildings? Haven't a clue." She held up her hands. "I'm being truthful."

"Then what's with the tunic and the chairs?" Bev asked.

"Well, *those* aren't involved, I can tell you that," Hendry said. "Or if they are, it's not my doing."

"Then what's the purpose?"

"Look, we've had something of an influx of soldiers lately, haven't we?" Hendry said. "Dag Flanigan is still mucking about the countryside, so I hear, not to mention that Claude fellow and Karolina Hunter. We had a blissful few years of *nobody* coming to town, and something seems to have changed, right?"

Bev nodded.

"Well, I feel as though I've been a little lucky." She adjusted her tunic. "Nobody's really noticed when I've befuddled them or kept them off my scent. But Flanigan presents a new challenge. I heard what happened with that ring."

One of Bev's guests had had a ring similar to Hendry's powers, and Flanigan had been able to thwart its powers with a magical bangle.

A bangle you saw in… Not helpful timing, Bev thought to herself.

"If he were to see me casting magic like that, I assume I would be in handcuffs like your lovely guest Bernie," Hendry said. "Especially since these soldiers aren't exactly *obvious* when they've come to town. Claude had us all fooled, as you recall."

"I do."

"So, over the winter, I found a way to *impart* my magic into inanimate objects. A potion that I can use in furniture varnish or, when it's done, the tanddaes wool tunic. That way, I still get the benefit of the magic without having to wield it myself."

"And you think that'll work?" Bev asked. "Flanigan was pretty quick on the uptake."

"Well, if he asks about it, I can point to the

chairs and tunics," she said. "Vehemently and horrifically denying I had any knowledge of the powers they possess."

And potentially getting Earl, Apolinary, and Bathilda in trouble. "I see."

"But we're getting off track. You think *I* had something to do with these incidents in town, and I'm telling you I didn't." She lifted a shoulder. "Therefore, we have nothing to discuss."

"I think it's no coincidence that your things were found in those places, though," Bev said. "Perhaps it's not you, but someone trying to get to you?"

"I had nothing in Alice's barn, Bev."

Well, that was true. She huffed, wishing she had a chair to slump into.

"But..." Hendry lifted her chin, as if being struck by an idea. "Perhaps you aren't completely off."

"What do you mean?"

"Well, what if whoever or whatever is destroying houses doesn't know what's going on?" Hendry said. "Assuming it is a person and not...well, not just a random fluke."

"How could they not know what's going on?"

"Not sure," Hendry said. "There are many explanations. But the one thing we do know is that each of the incidents happened near a large concentration of magic, right?"

Beasts and Baking

Bev opened her mouth to argue that the tanddaes were a bit far from Alice's barn, until she remembered the magical river flowing below Alice's property.

"It certainly appears that way," Bev said.

"Hm." Hendry sat back and steepled her fingers. "Then perhaps we should just start testing everyone in town. Expose them to high concentrations of magic and see what happens."

"*See what happens?*" Bev blinked. "That's a *horrible* idea."

"I'm not saying give them enough to destroy a building, but just enough to cause a small reaction." She flipped over the page, smiling to herself. "Really, Bev, I don't see why you think these mysteries are so difficult. I've all but solved it in the past five minutes."

She was certainly giving herself too much credit. "You really want to douse everyone in town with your magic?"

"My magic? Oh, no, dear. I don't have *nearly* enough for that."

"Don't you?" Bev tilted her head. On more than one occasion, Bev had personally witnessed Hendry spelling the entire town at once. "What about the chairs and the tunics?"

"That's *concentrated* magic. Spent most of the winter getting it into a form that was usable," Hendry said. "And the tanddaes wool isn't *my* magic, but I don't think Bathilda wants to trot them out like it's the Harvest Festival." She pursed her lips. "No, we're going to have to use something quite potent."

"What are you suggesting?"

"Well, I don't know many magical people in Pigsend," Hendry said. "But I'm sure you can find one or two who can lend some magic to our cause." She paused. "Maybe Allen Mackey could whip up something. His mother seemed to be magical. Maybe he's got it in him, too. He could whip up something delicious and potent, I'm sure."

He didn't have magic per se, but he *did* have a magical bauble that might work. And Bev *did* need to pop by and figure out what in the world was going on with him.

"So I ask Allen to make some magical pastries," Bev said. "How do I get them to the townsfolk? How do we even know if they have a reaction?"

"Simple. We test them all at once." She smiled. "I think, Bev, that this calls for a town meeting."

Chapter Fifteen

In Pigsend, there were only a few things everyone knew. One, stay out of Rosie Kelooke's yard or run the risk of her demonic chickens. And two, when someone called for a town meeting, it would be held that night—and everyone in town was expected to attend.

Bev left the mayor's office thinking of the long list of tasks on her plate, the first of which was to ask Allen if he'd be able to make some magical pastries. It was a big ask. At least a hundred and fifty folks would come—more if word got out about Alice's barn. Plus, Allen would have to use his bauble, which he'd likened to feeling like he'd gotten his mother back.

Not to mention the baker's strange behavior toward his girlfriend, so he might have his own issues going on.

"Either way," Bev said to Biscuit, "we're going to get to the bottom of things."

But when Bev got to the bakery, the doors were locked.

"Allen?" She rapped on the door. "Are you home?"

He hadn't dropped off pastries that morning, but Bev thought he might've been avoiding Vicky. She walked around to the back door and knocked again, raising her voice so it would carry to his second-floor bedroom.

"Allen? Don't tell me you've gone into the enchanted forest again."

She'd rather not have to search for him there, especially since the last time she'd gone, she'd witnessed Dag Flanigan arresting someone for illegally dealing in wyvern eggs.

She walked back around to the front then peered into the front windows. It looked completely deserted, like he hadn't been home in days.

Biscuit pawed at a piece of paper on the ground. Bev knelt and picked it up, recognizing Allen's scrawl.

Gone for the week.

"Well, thanks for letting us all know, Allen," Bev muttered.

The paper had something sticky on the back, perhaps an attempt to keep it on the window, but it clearly hadn't been strong enough. That certainly explained why he hadn't been by to check on Vicky, though it was strange he hadn't bothered to *tell* anyone (let alone his girlfriend) he was leaving. He didn't have any family out of town that he'd have to rush to tend to, and no business so urgent he couldn't at least tell Bev or even the Witzels where he was going.

"I do hope you're all right," Bev whispered.

It was very unlike him—at least the Allen Bev had come to know in the past few months. He'd been pulling down a tidy business with Bev's guests as well as Etheldra's tea shop, and he was well out from under the debts he'd accumulated while trying to find his footing after his mother's passing. He'd been happy, even, about his future with Vicky.

When did he leave?

The question sat uncomfortably in Bev's mind. Could *Allen* be the one causing the problems?

It was plausible, especially in light of Hendry's theory about the person not knowing they were responsible. She hadn't really elaborated beyond that, and Bev didn't really know enough about magical creatures to speculate. Up until now, he hadn't demonstrated any magic whatsoever, but his *mother* had definitely been blessed.

"No need to jump to conclusions," Bev said,

brushing imaginary dust off her pants. "There's probably a perfectly reasonable explanation for why he up and left so suddenly. Without telling anyone." She cleared her throat, remembering she was talking to herself. "Well."

Biscuit let out a low ruff.

"Suppose we need to find someone else to ask, then," Bev said. "Since our baker seems to have flown the coop."

Biscuit sat and tilted his head, his little eyebrow quirking in question.

"There might be a few options," Bev said, her hands on her hips. "Well, one, that I know of, who might be able to do what we're asking."

Biscuit wagged his tail.

"I wouldn't be too excited, B," Bev said with a sigh. "Because she's probably not going to be too thrilled to help us."

~

"Hmph. Sounds like a good way to destroy the town hall," Etheldra said with a glare. "Which would be fine by me. Gaudy, ugly building. Useful for nothing."

Etheldra had told Bev once that she had the preternatural ability to combine herbs and other plants in her teas, but Bev wasn't quite sure how that translated into spelling the entire village.

"So you can help?" Bev asked.

Bev had managed to get Etheldra to agree to

speak to her in private, but not without loud complaining that attracted the attention of everyone in the tearoom.

"Suppose I'll have to, seeing as Allen's skipped town for who-knows-why," Etheldra grumbled. "Having to serve day-old scones. Good thing they're supposed to be dry and crumbly."

"He didn't talk to you, either?" Bev frowned. Besides Bev, Etheldra was Allen's best customer. "Well, hopefully he'll be back soon, and there will be a good explanation."

"I wouldn't count on it." Etheldra walked to the wall of tea tins and tilted her head up. "Hendry says she can't do it?"

"She said there needed to be a concentration of magic, and she wasn't able to provide that," Bev said, watching her pull down a tin and sniff it.

"I'm sure." Etheldra rolled her eyes as she put the tin back. "I've seen her spell the entire town hall before. Don't know what she's on about, *can't use her magic*. Just doesn't want to be suspected, that's all."

Bev teetered on her toes for a moment, waiting for Etheldra to give her something. But she just kept smelling the tins and putting them back.

"Um." Bev cleared her throat after a long moment "What are you—?"

"Looking for the right thing, of course," Etheldra snapped. "This isn't an exact science, you know. Have to be careful you don't trigger someone to spew rainbows out of their…whatever."

"Is that possible?"

"Can't say I've seen it myself." She chuckled and found another tin. "Can't say I wouldn't mind seeing it. But if we're going to be spelling people—and we don't want to cause *too big* of a reaction, we'll have to pick just the right—ah!" She took another long inhale of the tin. "This'll do."

"What do I do with it?" Bev asked as Etheldra scooped the fragrant petals into a small bag.

"Hendry was right about one thing: ingestible magic is the way to go. It gets to the blood faster than through the skin or air." She tied the string on the bag and tossed it to Bev.

Bev inhaled. "Is this lavender?"

"Aye."

"What's special about lavender?" Bev asked.

"What's special about that rosemary in your garden?" Etheldra asked.

"Nothing." Bev lowered the bag. "Not that I'm aware of, anyway."

"So you say." Etheldra turned to put the tin back on the wall. "If I were you, I'd whip up something sweet and use this in a glaze."

"I'm not really the baking type," Bev said. Then, to Etheldra's quizzical expression, she added, "Baking sweets, I mean."

"Sweets, rosemary bread, it's all ingredients that

you mix together and put in a hot oven, isn't it?" She chuckled. "But if you feel woefully out of your depth, I'm sure Fernley has a recipe card somewhere in that shop. I remember her having a box of them, even."

"Yes, but Allen isn't home," Bev reminded her.

"Then help yourself to it."

"I don't know if he'd appreciate me taking one of his mother's cards."

"Well, then he shouldn't have left town when you needed magical scones baked, hm?" She adjusted her shawl as she walked out into the main room with another tin under her arm.

"W-wait." Bev pocketed the bag and ran after her. "You don't have any kind of recipe I could use?"

"If I did, I wouldn't be paying that Mackey boy to bring me sweets every morning, now would I?" The tea shop owner went to refill one of the canisters in the front of the store. "And I'll be sure to sit near the exit this evening, just in case you unleash a giant monster on the town."

Bev started. "Monster?"

"Well, what else could it be? Something nobody sees that can grow as big as a house? Seems monstrous to me." She spoke plainly as she filled the canister. "There's a reason I haven't been lacing my own teas with it lately. Never know who might be having a bad couple of weeks."

~

Biscuit was certainly interested in the bag of lavender, which told Bev all she needed to know about its potency. She placed the bag way out of his (very tenacious) reach, and pointedly instructed him to leave it alone.

"I'll let you have any that are left over," Bev said, wagging her finger at him. "But don't you touch this until then, understand?"

He whined but dropped his head.

"Now." She put her hands on her hips and let out a sigh. "I suppose we need to break into Allen's bakery, don't we?"

Rosemary bread Bev could make with her eyes closed. Cinnamon rolls, too, were quite easy to make (as they used the same dough). But anything beyond that went outside the scope of Wim McKee's tutelage, and Bev had never seen the need to learn more, what with Fernley, then Allen across the street.

Bev headed to the bakery's back door, turning over empty flour bags, rocks, and anything else in search of the spare key Allen had told her he kept. She finally found it under the mat, and with an unsettled feeling in her stomach, let herself in.

"Allen?" Bev called. "Are you here?"

If he was, he hadn't been baking. There was a distinctive chill to the air that only came from several days of no fires in the oven. Everything was impeccably clean, too, so it didn't seem like he'd dashed out in a hurry. More like a very planned trip.

The clock on the wall chimed, reminding Bev that she *was* on something of a time limit. She rifled through the boxes and tins under the counter but found nothing except extra sugar and sprinkles. She headed toward the kitchen, opening cabinets and boxes.

"Where do you keep the recipes?" Bev muttered to herself.

She stopped, glancing upward. Would he keep them in his apartment upstairs?

"Well, we are friends," Bev said, walking up the back stairwell. "Allen, if you're home, I'm terribly sorry."

She let herself into the small living space. There were two chairs next to the hearth, a table in what could only be described as the kitchen corner, and a twin bed made and covered with one of Merv's quilts. Next to the bed was a bedside table with a single drawer.

Allen had once said he kept the magical bauble next to his bed, because the magic reminded him of his mother. Perhaps he kept her recipe cards there, too.

Bev held her breath and opened the drawer. There was a box with cards inside covered in Fernley's handwriting—

—but no bauble.

Bev searched the whole drawer, even inside the

recipe card box, but the bright green, marble-sized magical object was nowhere to be found. Not that Allen was under any obligation to keep it in the spot he'd told her, but something felt *off* about it not being here. Had he taken it with him on his impromptu journey?

Or did the bauble trigger him into transforming into a monster, and he skipped town with it?

"Allen, what in the world are you up to?" Bev muttered, picking up the recipe cards and sifting through them. Every single recipe Fernley had ever baked seemed to be here. From delicate pastries to the solstice walnut loaf to the breakfast biscuits that had given Bev's laelaps his distinctive name, they were all here, in loopy handwriting that made Bev smile in memory of the affable baker.

Midway through the deck, Bev found a recipe for basic scones that would do the trick. She put the rest of the cards back the way she'd found them. Allen would (most likely) not be cross with her for breaking into his place, if one could even call it that, but she didn't want to leave a mess.

She did, however, snag a pound of sugar, as well as eggs, buttermilk, and pearl ash, which was used to leaven dough in place of yeast. Her arms full, she toddled back to the inn to start the process.

She placed Fernley's card in the center of her kitchen table, making sure it was away from any flour or flying dough, and read the instructions three times. She started with the usual ingredients—flour and sugar, plus the pearl ash, and, although Etheldra hadn't said to, she sprinkled some of the lavender leaves into the scones themselves. To that, she added cold butter that she'd kept down at the bottom of her root cellar and mixed it in until the butter resembled small peas, as Fernley's card instructed.

In another bowl, she whisked buttermilk and an egg then poured that into the mix, turning it over until it became a sticky mess. It was a different texture than her rosemary bread. She shaped the dough into three large, flat circles and cut wedges out of them, placing them on her oven pan. When all was said and done, she had thirty-six scones.

"This may take longer than I thought," Bev said, looking down at Biscuit, who was on his hind legs sniffing the dough.

With an eye on the time (and on dinner), Bev doubled the next batch, then made one more doubled set. While the scones baked in batches, she set to making the glaze. As Etheldra had instructed, she put a large pot of milk on the stove under low heat and let the remaining tea leaves soak for fifteen minutes. Then, she added lemon juice and all the sugar she had left, which turned the milk into a delicious-smelling glaze.

"What in the world is cooking in here?" Rita, Janet, and Gladys came into the kitchen, their noses tilted toward the ceiling like Biscuit's.

"Oh—um." Bev had a moment of panic. Would the grannies undo her hard work? Their appetite seemed to be insatiable, and they'd never stopped long enough to ask if they could eat Allen's pastries. "These are for the town meeting tonight."

"Town meeting?" Rita asked.

Janet tilted her head. "What in the world is that?"

"And why are you baking for it?" Gladys finished.

"Well, the mayor is concerned about all the buildings being destroyed," Bev said, keenly watching them for any signs of guilt. "Wants to get some feedback and ideas for what might be causing it." She swallowed. "I'll be bringing all these scones to pass out. To be…nice."

Gladys hovered around the ones cooling on the rack but didn't take one. "You do too much, Bev."

Janet tutted. "Just work yourself to the bone."

"Do you ever take a day off?" Rita put her hand on Bev's table.

"Sometimes," Bev said, sensing that she wouldn't have to say anything to the grannies to keep them from taking one. Was that suspicious? "You're welcome to come to the town meeting, if you like. I'll warn you that it's quite boring, and we can go off on tangents that last until the wee hours of the morning. But it can be entertaining. And if you have any idea of what's destroying buildings in town, we'd be all ears."

They shared a look then brightened. "We'd be ecstatic to attend."

Chapter Sixteen

The grannies, who'd graciously offered to help bring the baskets of scones to the meeting hall, settled themselves in the front row, though Bev noted they didn't take a pastry for themselves. They didn't offer any suggestions or hints that they knew the culprit behind the destruction, and Bev wasn't confident they'd volunteer any new information during the town meeting. But she was somewhat glad they were there—especially if the scones prompted another incident.

Bev wasn't sure what sort of magic Etheldra had put in the lavender, but when a little glaze got on her finger, magic buzzed in her veins.

She placed the baskets by the front door and

waited, gazing at the cathedral ceiling above and hoping it wasn't about to be a treasured memory. If they were dealing with *monsters*, as Etheldra said, then there was no telling what they might unleash.

Hendry arrived, looking impeccable in a red tunic with matching lipstick. Bev gave her a once-over, wondering if there wasn't any *additional* magic in her vibrant lips.

"I take it those are your mysterious guests," Hendry said, nodding toward the grannies. "They do seem rather elderly for the work they've been doing."

"You'd think," Bev said, offering Hendry one of the full baskets. "Scone?"

"Heavens, no." She sniffed. "I can feel the magic from here. But they'll do just fine to suss out whomever is wreaking havoc on the town."

"And you're sure you want to unleash whatever it is while we're all in here?" Bev asked, looking up at the ceiling. "I don't think the grannies can rebuild the town hall without scaffolding."

"Yes, yes, of course," Hendry said, plastering on a smile. "Now buck up. Here come the townsfolk."

They emerged from the dark, grumbling about a town meeting when it was still so cold outside. Bev kept quiet, watching Hendry greet each person.

"Evening, Gore. So good to see you, Sonny. Please, take one. Yes, you need one." She smiled at Trent Scrawl, who'd declined to take one, and the old farmer's eyes glazed over as he took the proffered pastry. "It's good for your health."

"Oh, all right." He took a bite. "Delicious."

"I thought you didn't have enough magic to spell people," Bev muttered as he walked away.

"I have a little to spare," she said, handing another to Bardoff as he walked in. "Good evening. Lovely to see you."

"Scones?" Bardoff inhaled. "Are you getting into baking sweets, Bev?"

"Trying out something new," Bev said. "Might help keep everyone in a good mood this evening."

"Doubtful," Earl said, helping himself to one and taking a big bite. "Whole town's on edge again. Like when those sinkholes started. Nobody knows who's next."

Bev watched him carefully, not sure when or how the magic would take effect. The room was starting to fill up, and the trail of crumbs made Bev nervous. What if they unleashed something no one could control?

"Oh, don't look so ill, Bev, this is working," Hendry said. "Not one demonstration of magic yet."

"You think it would happen so quickly?" Bev muttered as Rosie Kelooke took one to her seat.

"I've had a bite. Trust me, it would be quick." She waved at Bathilda, who came storming up with a suspicious look on her face. "Good to see you,

Bathilda. Not sure you were going to make it."

"And why wouldn't I?" She grunted, giving Bev the stink eye. "What's this all about?"

"Just trying to get to the bottom of the destruction," Hendry said. "I'm sure you'll be happy to speak to the crowd about what you witnessed—or rather, didn't witness—the day Alice's barn collapsed."

"Didn't see a thing." Bathilda eyed the scones. "And what are these? Can't remember a time we had baked goods at a town meeting."

"I asked Bev to whip them up. Seemed like we could all use a nice treat in the midst of all this mess." Hendry's smile broadened. "Please, try one."

Bev was certain the old farmer wouldn't, but she snatched one off the top and tore into it as she walked to her seat. Bev held her breath, watching her before Hendry hissed at her.

"Clearly, it's not Bathilda," the mayor muttered. "If it were, she'd probably be triggered by that large collection of magical sheep in her yard, wouldn't she?"

Bev supposed that made sense. "Are they still there, you think? She said she was hoping to sell them."

"I'm sure I don't know anything about them." Hendry turned to the latest arrivals, the Witzels. "Good to see you, Vellora. Ida. You're looking well after your holiday to the south. Have a scone."

"Oh, don't mind if I do," Ida said. "Bev, are you baking sweets now?"

"Allen leaves for a few nights, and you take his job," Vellora said with a good-natured smile.

"Do either of you know where he went in such a hurry?" Bev asked.

They shook their heads. "Just that we haven't seen him," Ida said.

"Hurry, hurry, to your seats," Hendry said.

Bev scanned the dark, empty streets for anyone else as she glanced at the clock. Nearly seven.

Pip and Holly Norris shuffled in and needed some goading to take a pastry. The same for Apolinary, who came in after them.

"Shop is nearly ready. Those grannies are good at what they do," Apolinary said.

"So I've heard," Hendry said. "Scone?"

The seamstress took one, going to sit next to the Norrises before tucking into the scone.

"Well, it's not them," Hendry muttered. "Suppose that's everyone. Shall we get going?"

"How do you—?" Bev began, but Hendry was already halfway up the middle walkway to the front of the room.

"Did everyone get a scone?" Hendry asked the crowd when she reached the front. "Oh, Herman, make sure you pop over and get one. They're practically divine. Yes, yes, go get one now. Pass it along." She smiled happily at the crowd. "Everyone got one? Good." She sat in her chair. "Now, let's begin."

The mayor's magic coated the room, quieting the conversations. Bev held her breath, waiting for someone to become something else or roar or spew fire or any manner of horrific things, but all that looked back were mildly bored faces.

"We're here because of these new incidents happening all over town," Hendry continued. "I'd like to open the floor to Bev, who's been looking into this for us." She smiled. "Bev?"

Bev rose, having realized in just that moment that she hadn't thought out what she'd say—hadn't even considered she'd be called on at all.

"Well, as we know, the first incident was at Earl's workshop, which burned down. The second was out in Alice's barn. And just recently, Apolinary's shop." She gestured toward the room. "It's not real clear what the pattern is."

"Do we have any theories?" Hendry asked.

"A couple," Bev said. "But I'd like to see if anyone in town has seen anything suspicious first."

"I saw something odd over at Herman Monday's place," Trent Scrawl said, standing with a look.

Bev rolled her eyes. "The feud's back on, is it?"

"Well, yes, but this time I'm serious!" Trent said. "There was a group of strange-looking people walking by his place late at night."

"And what were you doing up by my place late

at night?" Herman said, rising. "Better not be stealing my soil again, you cur."

"I can take as much as I want, since it's *cheatin'* soil anyway!" Trent shot back.

"All right, all right," Bev said, holding up her hands. "What did the people look like?"

"Well, I couldn't tell in the dark, but there were five of 'em. Skulking around like they were up to no good," Herman continued.

"I'm sure *whoever it was* is long gone by now," Bathilda said, her head barely visible behind Rosie.

Bev nodded. Bathilda's farm butted up to Herman's as well as Alice's. Perhaps the people "skulking about" were the sellers taking her illegal sheep.

"Anyone else?"

"Well, I think I speak for the town when I say we should be taking a closer look at those kids who were hanging around my workshop," Earl said, rising.

"They had nothing to do with it," Holly Norris said, standing on the other side of the room. "Maybe you should've been more careful with your spirits."

"Spirits don't just spontaneously combust, Holly," Earl shot back. "Someone set my warehouse on fire. Now, whether they meant to or not is another story, but—"

"PJ and his friends had nothing to do with it,"

she said. "I can vouch for his whereabouts. *And* his friends."

Gilda cleared her throat as she stood. "Besides that, the kids were in school when Alice's barn was destroyed. And that, at least, wasn't set on fire."

Bev scanned the room to see if Vicky would stand up for her little brother, but she wasn't in the room—nor was her brother. Allen made up the last of the missing townsfolk.

"None of the buildings that've collapsed since your workshop were set on fire," Holly said.

"So maybe it was your boy for my place, and something else for the others," Earl said with a wave of his hand.

"All right, all right," Hendry said, as Pip stood angrily. "Let's not cast stones without evidence. We're here to get to the bottom of things, not get into fistfights."

"And most likely, it's one culprit," Bev said.

"What do you think it is?" Bardoff asked. "You said you have theories. Share them. Might help us know what to look for."

Bev rubbed the back of her head. She wasn't planning on scaring the group—and seeing how easily Earl and Pip had almost gotten into it, the town was clearly on edge.

The air vibrated as a roar echoed through the room, sending people to their feet in panic and fear. For a second, Bev feared they might stampede out, but Hendry rose and held up her hands.

"Calm yourselves," she demanded.

The movement stopped, and every face turned to the mayor.

"Now, let's queue up and see what's going on in an *orderly fashion*," she said—and those in the meeting space did as instructed. Bev sidled up beside Hendry as they followed the line out the door.

"What was that about not having enough magic to spell the room?" Bev muttered.

"Well, you know, when push comes to shove…"

~

It didn't take them long to find out what new calamity had befallen the town. Just across from the town hall, Bardoff's beloved one-room school was in pieces all over the town square. A hush fell over the crowd as they surveyed the damage.

"Oh, Bardoff," Ida said, placing her hand on the desolate schoolteacher's shoulder.

"Don't you worry," Rita said, assuming her usual stance of picking up the pieces of the school. "We'll have you back to teaching in no time."

"Right you are, sister," Janet said. "Earl, how much wood do we have left?"

"Not much," the carpenter replied. "Used most of it on Apolinary's shop."

"Then we'll have to make another trip to Middleburg."

"What about the town?" Rosie said. "There's something out there that keeps destroying buildings. Are we just going to stand here and let it get away?"

"You're welcome to go after it," Hendry said with a smile. "But I would go in groups, just to be safe. I think we all heard just how *large* that creature was. No telling if they're dangerous."

"So it is a creature, then?" Rosie Kelooke said. "And Sheriff Rustin out of town!"

"Not as if he'd do much about it anyway," Ida muttered.

"We're not sure what it is," Bev said. "But we do know that everyone who attended the town meeting *can't* be involved, right?"

The townsfolk eyed each other warily.

"Right?" Bev said.

"Suppose you've got a point there," Rosie said, inching away from Bathilda.

"So I think the best option is for us to return to our homes. If you notice anyone who wasn't in attendance tonight, you might ask them what they were doing this evening," Hendry said. "Politely, of course. And be sure to tell Bev about any developments."

"How do we know we're safe in our own homes?"

"Vicky Hamblin nearly died in Apolinary's shop!"

"She was fine," Apolinary said. "Just had a little

shock, that's all."

"How do we know *you* aren't responsible?" Rosie said, glaring at Apolinary. "It was your shop that collapsed!"

Arguments began breaking out again, and Bev looked at Hendry for help. The mayor let out a frustrated sigh, rolled her eyes, and put her hands to her mouth.

"Go home," she said, and Bev felt the tingling to return to the inn. "There's nothing to be done about this right now. Return to your residences and go to bed."

It took a bit, but the townsfolk finally broke away and headed back toward their respective houses. Even Ida and Vellora, who seemed to want to stay and chat with Bev, couldn't resist the suggestion from the mayor. The only ones who could, it seemed, were Bev, the grannies, and Bardoff.

"What am I going to tell the children?" he said, sounding a little lost. "If there's not a schoolhouse, the parents might decide there shouldn't be any school."

"The town hall is right there," Bev said.

"Absolutely not," Hendry said. "There's far too much important business going on there for you to be teaching there." She tilted her head. "But the inn is fairly empty, is it not? Apolinary said the grannies were nearly finished rebuilding her shop."

Beasts and Baking

Bev scowled. "It is, but—"

"Then it's settled. Bardoff, be sure to tell the children of the new location. I'm sure it'll be nice to have some company at the inn, Bev."

"You've certainly got a way with the people," Rita said, walking up to the mayor with a bright smile on her face.

"Pigsend is lucky to have you," added Gladys.

"Amazing how they listen!" Janet said.

"Yes, well…" Hendry cleared her throat. "You've been an invaluable asset to Pigsend, and I must thank you for all you've done for us during this time of chaos."

"Nonsense."

"Happy to do it."

"Least we can do for such a hospitable town."

"But if you'll give Bev and me a moment, we need to discuss what just happened." Hendry's eyes flashed, and the tingling increased.

"No need to use that magic on us, dear," Gladys said.

Rita nodded. "Got the message loud and clear."

"You go back into that town hall and chat. We've got to do some measuring so we can leave for Middleburg in the morning." Janet waved them toward the town meeting hall. "Off you pop!"

Hendry seemed annoyed to be directed by these out-of-towners but still followed Bev back into the town hall. There were leftover scones scattered on the benches, and an odd amount of energy permeating the room. It seemed almost too quiet after the spectacle of the town meeting earlier.

"The only townsfolk I didn't see were Allen Mackey and Vicky Hamblin." Hendry handed Bev the list she'd been working on. "I also wrote down a litany of folks who didn't touch their scones, but I suppose *that* is a moot point now."

"Seems to be the case." Bev picked up an uneaten scone and put it back in her basket, intending to bring it back to the inn for Biscuit. "I thought for sure we'd find our culprit tonight."

"Oh, I didn't," she said with a sly grin. "You see, Bev, I assumed that our person *wouldn't* show up. You can't be causing this much destruction about town and not have any idea why. So the ones who weren't here…we need to find out why."

"Allen is out of town," Bev said.

"Is he? Or is he simply hiding his true form?" Hendry asked. "Either way, I think you should start with him—and his girlfriend, too."

Chapter Seventeen

Allen absolutely *couldn't* be the one Bev was looking for. For one, Bev had seen him in his bakery when Alice's barn had collapsed. But Vicky?

Vicky was another story.

Bev lay in her bed, Biscuit's quiet snores echoing against the walls, as she thought about the potentially dangerous creature sleeping three doors down. Could Vicky really be a monster in disguise?

If it even was a monster. But that roar had been pretty monstrous-sounding.

The evidence was starting to pile up. She'd been *inside* Apolinary's shop when it collapsed and saw no one else. Perhaps even handling Bathilda's magic-infused fabric as she cut and sewed the pattern. And ever since, she'd taken ill. Had she come out of the inn, intending on coming to the town meeting, but instead transformed into a monster that had stomped out the schoolhouse?

It wasn't the first sign of Vicky's magical abilities, either. She was in tune with nature, having a preternatural obsession with trees, plants, and the delicate balance of the environment. Was that a precursor to her transformation, or something else?

There were holes in the theory, of course. By all accounts, she was nowhere near Alice's barn when it collapsed. She didn't have any reason to be, either. But Bev had been surprised to hear about Hendry being at Bathilda's, so perhaps Vicky had another reason to be out that way, too.

When morning broke, and the inn *hadn't* been destroyed by something magical and fierce, Bev set to her chores, keeping the kitchen door propped open to hear from Allen. There hadn't been any lights on at the bakery when Bev had returned after the town meeting, but that didn't mean he hadn't come back sometime in the night. Bev did have a few scones left over, so she placed those out for anyone who might want one.

Apolinary arrived bright and early to retrieve her fabric, along with a heartfelt thank you to Bev for allowing her to work in the inn.

"I didn't do a thing, but glad I could help." She nodded toward the stairs. "Is Vicky coming to work today?"

"Who knows?" Apolinary sighed. "She looked so miserable yesterday. I'm sure she's still moping today. But sooner or later, she's going to have to drag herself out of bed and come back to work."

She sounded much less sympathetic than the day before. Bev couldn't really blame her; there seemed to be a lot of work to get done, and if Vicky's only ailment was a broken heart...

Or was it?

"Say, Apolinary," Bev began, "Vicky hasn't been acting strangely, has she?"

"Other than the usual?" Apolinary chuckled. "No. If anything, she's been less flighty than her normal self. Hasn't been on about the birds and trees and the way the plants talk to one another."

"I see." Bev straightened the log book on the counter. "Speaking of that flightiness, any clue what it might—"

"Oh, Bev. You don't think Vicky's the one terrorizing the town, do you?" Apolinary said with a chuckle. "I mean, I can't say I believe *anyone* is doing that, but Vicky? Come now."

"It's possible," Bev said. "Especially with her lying about."

"I haven't been *lying* about. And I'm certainly *not* transforming into a giant monster." Vicky appeared at the top of the stairs wearing an actual shirt and pants, for once. She still seemed pale and miserable as she slowly walked down the stairs. She grimaced as she sat, as if her head hurt.

"Good to see you up and about," Apolinary said.

"Suppose I should get back to work, hm?" Vicky said with a sad sigh as she pulled the fabric toward her. "These dresses aren't going to make themselves."

"Would be nice if they could," Apolinary said with a small smile. She reached across and patted Vicky on the knee. "I'm glad you're feeling better."

"I'm not, really," Vicky said. "But it wouldn't be right to leave you to all this by yourself."

"Why don't I put on a kettle for the two of you?" Bev said, eager to keep Vicky at the inn a little longer. "If the shop's not quite ready yet, you can stay and get a little work done this morning. There's no rush to leave."

"Don't trouble yourself, Bev," Vicky said. "You've done enough for my brother and me. Even if you think I'm turning into something...what was it? Monstrous?"

"You missed the town meeting," Bev said.

"I was asleep," Vicky replied.

"Well, you also missed that *another* building got destroyed," Apolinary said.

Vicky furrowed her brow. "Which one?"

"The schoolhouse," Bev said, walking to the window and pulling back the curtain. "Which means we should be getting a gaggle of schoolchildren any moment now."

"Perhaps we should leave, then," Apolinary said.

"Nonsense." Bev waved her off. "Plenty of room for everybody."

"I might actually take you up on that tea, then," Vicky said, touching her head. "Got something of an ache."

"I'll get right on that," Bev said, walking into the kitchen.

The kettle went over the fire, and Bev put two cups and the teapot on a tray. She went to her stores of teas and found her usual batch was running low. Another trip to Etheldra's would be in order.

Unless… Bev turned to the bag of magical lavender she'd been given the day before. There was plenty for a full pot, but she didn't want to risk giving either woman more than a small taste. She'd already had to rebuild the inn once in the past year.

The kettle whistled, startling Bev. She pulled it off the fire and set it beside her trusty teapot. She filled the pot with the last of her normal tea, plus a small sprinkle of Etheldra's special blend.

She put the top on the teapot and walked out from the kitchen, stopping short. Vicky was chomping down on a scone from the night before, marveling to Apolinary, who was also nibbling on a piece, about how delicious it was.

"Bev, I don't know *what* you put in these," she

said, her mouth full. "But I can't get enough!"

Bev held her breath, watching Vicky for what felt like an eternity. The other woman was oblivious, enjoying the delectable scone with the sweet topping while working on a vibrant green skirt.

"What is it?" Apolinary asked. "You look like you've seen a ghost!"

"Oh, clearly not," Bev said with a nervous chuckle as she placed the tea down. The more time passed without either of them spewing fire or growing wings or some other horrible appendage, the easier she breathed. So much for *that* theory.

The door flew open, and Bev once again almost jumped out of her skin. This time, a parade of kids came marching in, followed by Bardoff. He was carrying a thick stack of books and kicked the door closed behind him.

"Ah, Bev! So glad you're here," he said. "Oh, I didn't realize you'd be here, too, Apolinary. Suppose this is the repository for all the poor folks who are waiting for their houses to be rebuilt."

"Good thing it's the quiet season," Bev said. Now that she'd tested Vicky and Apolinary, there didn't seem a reason to keep them in earshot. "Room five is empty if you two want a quiet place to work."

"I think I'd rather sit and listen," Apolinary said.

"Yes, me, too," Vicky said, watching her brother with a wary expression. "Might help the day go faster."

"Well, happy to oblige," Bardoff said, dropping the books on the table with a loud *bang*. "Find a seat, children, and we'll get started."

There seemed to be even fewer kids than before, only seven today. They pulled the chairs out, loudly scraping the floor, and sat with various stages of interest.

Bev kept to the kitchen, but left the door open to watch. Bardoff really was quite bright, jumping from astronomy to mathematics to history to literature with ease. The children of Pigsend were getting quite an education from him, but as much as she hated to admit it, most of what he was teaching them seemed inapplicable to the life of a farmer. She'd probably never use the knowledge of how to chart the stars or the importance of such-and-such duke to the history of the kingdom. But it was interesting to know, and it did help the morning's chores go faster.

"Now, children," Bardoff said with a bright tone. "Yesterday, we were discussing the finer points of astronomy. Who can give me the name of one of the constellations we learned about?"

No one raised their hands, so Vicky cleared her throat. "I'm sure Grant knows the answer."

"Guh, *Vicky*." Grant grunted. "Why are you here?"

"Because our home was destroyed," she replied

with a raised brow. "Well? Go on. Answer him."

Grant muttered something that Bev didn't catch, earning a pleased sound from his teacher. "Great work. And PJ, what's another constellation nearby?"

He shrugged, and Apolinary hissed at him. "Don't be rude, PJ."

"Not being *rude*," he shot back. "And mind your own business, Auntie."

"I'll tell your mother," she said.

"Ah, ladies," Bardoff said lightly. "Perhaps it might be best if you left the questioning up to me. I'm sure PJ and Grant would learn better without the added pressure of their families watching."

Apolinary stabbed the fabric with her sewing needle, watching her nephew warily. Vicky, too, seemed a little too interested in her brother. But both remained quiet.

"Now." Bardoff cleared his throat. "Where were we?"

A loud gasp echoed through the room, catching everyone's attention. Bev's gaze flew to Vicky, whose whole body had gone as stiff and rigid as if she'd been dunked in cold water. The blood drained from her face as she slowly put down the tunic she was working on.

"Vicky?" Bev asked, walking out into the front room, fearing the worst. How long would it take the grannies to rebuild an entire inn?

Beasts and Baking

"What is it?" Apolinary asked.

"That little..." The blood returned to Vicky's face with a vengeance as her cheeks turned dark. She angrily threw aside her half-finished tunic and stormed toward the door.

"She's gonna murder him," Apolinary said, putting aside her tunic (albeit much more gently than Vicky).

"Murder..." Bev followed Apolinary's gaze to the open door and the figure in the bakery across the street. "Oh, goodness."

The two hurried across the street just as Vicky exploded.

"You've got a lot of nerve showing up here!"

Allen abruptly dropped the cupcake pan he was holding, and the white batter flew across the floor. He put his hand to his heart, taking a step back. "Vicky, you scared the daylights out of me."

Vicky's chest went up and down as Apolinary gently took her by the arm. "Now, Vicky, why don't we see if there's a logical explanation for—"

But Vicky wasn't having that. "It's been *days* since I nearly *died,* and you haven't even bothered to come see me."

"Wait, what?" Allen caught Bev's expression, his eyes widening. "What happened? You almost died?"

"You don't even *care*!" Vicky cried, walking right up to the counter and grabbing a roll out of the basket. She chucked it at her (perhaps former?)

boyfriend's head then chucked another, and would've gone for a third had Apolinary not snatched the basket out of arm's reach.

"Why don't we head back to the inn?" she said, pulling Vicky away from the artillery. "I think you've made your point."

"Vicky, I didn't know—I've been out of town!" Allen said. "Can someone *please* tell me what's going on?"

"What's going on is we're *done*, Allen," Vicky said, large tears leaking down her face. "I never want to see you again!"

And with that, she turned on her heel and ran back toward the inn, her face buried in her hands. Apolinary looked between Bev and a dumbfounded Allen for a moment before following her assistant.

Allen jumped as the door closed, turning to Bev with confusion plain on his face. "What did I do?"

"I think it's what you *didn't* do," Bev said. "You should go talk with her."

"Best to let her cool off," he said. To Bev's curious expression, he added, "This isn't the first time she's threatened to break up with me. Or lobbed baked goods at my head."

"Might be the last time, Allen," Bev said. "Where in the world have you been?"

"That's, uh…" His face reddened. "That's my business, Bev."

Bev pursed her lips.

"It's nothing bad, I promise. And I'll tell you eventually, just not… Not now," he said, holding up his hands. "Now will you *please* tell me what tried to kill my girlfriend while I was gone? And why she's somehow upset with *me* about it?"

"Put on a kettle," Bev said with a sigh. "You've got a lot to catch up on."

Bev told Allen about the two latest incidents and about serving magical pastries to the town with no results (along with an apology for breaking into his home and snagging his mother's card). To his credit, Allen listened without reacting, though he clicked his tongue when she told him that Vicky was staying across the street.

"No wonder she's so cross with me. Suppose nobody told her I was out of town?"

"The better question is why didn't you?" Bev asked.

His cheeks reddened. "Well, I didn't think I'd be gone that long… Besides that, I passed by the seamstress shop early this morning on my way back into town, and it looked…" He let out a sigh. "The grannies got to it, didn't they?"

Bev nodded. "Had it back up in two days."

"Well, she can hardly expect me to have known that," Allen said.

"I think she expected you to tell her you were leaving town," Bev said. "Why all the secrecy?"

"I promise, as soon as I'm ready to share, I will."

"Doesn't involve you turning into a giant beast and stomping on buildings, does it?" Bev asked.

"Are you...?" He stared at her. "You don't possibly think..."

"I think that someone who wasn't sitting in the town meeting last night destroyed the schoolhouse," Bev said. "And to my count, that number is just you and Vicky."

He swallowed. "It's not me, I can assure you of that. I wasn't even in town until early this morning."

"Then perhaps your hotheaded girlfriend is the one doing it," Bev said. "She was in the seamstress shop, and ever since has been moping around the inn. Looks pale, miserable, peaky. I thought it was just a broken heart, but now I'm not so sure."

"It's not Vicky," Allen said. "I know for a fact that she was with me when Earl's shop went up in flames."

"What about Alice's barn? The schoolhouse?" Bev tilted her head. "Maybe Earl's shop *was* the damn kids and—"

"Were there kids at the town meeting?" Allen asked.

"Well, no, but—"

"Then who's to say it wasn't one of them?"

Bev opened and closed her mouth. She hadn't considered that. "But what would the kids be doing near Alice's barn?"

"You know they get into all sorts of trouble," Allen said. "Roam the town like a bunch of thieves. I see Grant all the time when he's told Vicky's he's in school. Wouldn't surprise me if one of them is turning into a building-smashing monster."

"I don't think we should pin this on a moral failing," Bev said. "Whoever this is happening to… they probably either don't know or they're scared."

"And what do you propose to do once you find this…thing?" Allen asked. "You're not the sort of person who's equipped to handle a creature capable of smashing a barn."

Bev didn't know the answer to that, but she felt compelled to see this through to the end. "I think it's more important to *find* them first. It seems the transformation is triggered by magic—lots of it. If we find the person, we could tell them what to look out for. Help them keep from turning into a monster."

"And what if it isn't triggered by magic, but something else? What if this is all building up to some giant creature who'll destroy the town? What then?"

"I don't know," Bev said. "But we'll cross that bridge when we come to it."

Chapter Eighteen

Allen promised Bev that he'd smooth things over with Vicky as soon as she cooled off a bit, so Bev returned to the inn, ready to help in that endeavor, but the scorned lover was nowhere to be found. Apolinary was alone, working on the same tunic she'd been at before the chaos began.

"Where's Vicky?" Bev asked.

"Upstairs crying her eyes out," Apolinary said, pulling the thread through the tunic. "Poor thing could barely string two words together. You know, they've been on and off a lot, but I think this time, they're off for good."

"Allen doesn't seem to think so," Bev said, a little annoyed at her neighbor for being so cavalier about his girlfriend's feelings. "Assured me he'll be able to smooth things over with her."

"Allen might want to rethink that," Apolinary muttered.

Bev left the seamstress to her work, as she had dinner to get started. She popped over to the butchers—giving Ida all the details on the fight, which had been audible from across the street—and returned to the inn to work on her bread and side dishes.

The front door to the inn opened, and Bev leaned out to see who'd walked in. But it wasn't Allen; Vicky's brother had returned from wherever he'd run off to after class. He ignored Apolinary and walked right up to the basket of scones that had been untouched all morning, snatching one and taking a big bite.

"Hey, Grant?" Bev asked. "Mind coming in here for a minute?"

Based on his expression, he most certainly *did* mind being called into the kitchen but obliged anyway. "What?"

Bev cleared her throat. "Just curious where you were last night."

"Nowhere." *Munch, munch.* "None of your business anyway."

"What about Vicky?" Bev asked. "She didn't come to the town meeting."

"That's because she's all torn up about Allen.

Good riddance if you ask me." *Munch, munch.* "Got any more of these scones?"

"In the basket," Bev said. "Those were from the town meeting last night. Any chance you or your friends—"

"We ain't got nothing to do with these buildings getting destroyed," he said, his lip curling in a snarl. "And you'd better stop asking or else—"

"Or else what?" Bev asked, a fake smile on her face.

At the hearth, Biscuit raised his head and growled.

Grant glanced at the laelaps and swallowed the rest of the scone. "Nothing. Just leave us alone. We didn't do anything."

And with that, he turned on his heel and disappeared through the door, grabbing the last two scones on his way out.

"If he turns into a giant creature that destroys the inn tonight, I'm gonna be real mad," Bev said to Biscuit, who let out a low sniff. "Vicky's one thing. But if it's her snotty little brother…"

~

Hours passed and there didn't seem to be any new destructive forces in town, so Bev was reasonably confident Grant wasn't the monster. Or maybe he'd had the courtesy to transform in a large open field.

The grannies, however, arrived with great news

Beasts and Baking

—with Earl's help (and yet another trip to Middleburg for more wood), they'd finished rebuilding Apolinary's shop. The seamstress was overjoyed to hear that, and looking at the amount of fabric scraps on the floor of the inn, Bev was pretty happy about it, too.

"Good timing, too. We've got to get to work on your schoolhouse, Bardoff," Rita said, patting the teacher on the back. "Those children need somewhere to learn, don't they?"

"If I even have children left to teach," he said glumly. "I don't know if you noticed, Bev, but our numbers keep dwindling. I doubt Grant and PJ would've shown up had Vicky and Apolinary not been here."

"Apolinary, PJ said he was your nephew?" Bev asked.

She nodded. "Holly's my sister."

"Such a small town," Gladys said. "Lovely when everyone's related, isn't it?"

"Makes it so much easier to know who's who!" Janet replied.

"On occasion," Bev said. "Sometimes, I think people would rather not acknowledge their family." Etheldra and Ida came to mind, as did the farmer Grant Klose.

"Speaking of family," Rita said, looking up at the stairs, "where is that lovely assistant of yours? I'd love to tell her she and her brother are able to move back into their apartment tomorrow."

"Upstairs," Apolinary said.

"Oh, dear, has she taken ill again?" Gladys asked.

"Of a broken heart, yes," Bev said.

"Well, that just won't do, will it?" Janet stood. "Let me see if I can't convince her to come down and eat. Can't mend a broken heart on an empty stomach."

"Hear, hear!" Rita said.

"I don't think—" Bev started, but Janet was already halfway up the stairs. Bev didn't think it was possible to get Vicky out of bed, but five minutes later, both Janet and Vicky emerged, the latter looking miserable but still willing to come down.

"I don't want to talk about it," Vicky said to Bev as she took an empty bowl.

"You certainly don't have to," Bev said gently, handing her a second slice of rosemary bread. "But if you want—"

"I don't." She sniffed. "We're done. I mean it this time."

Bev nodded, keeping her thoughts to herself, and letting Vicky eat her dinner in silence. The grannies took up chattering with Apolinary, who was awfully grateful to them for their help. Bev scanned the room, noting Grant hadn't reappeared since his storm-out earlier in the day.

Almost on cue, the door opened again, but a

different kind of destructive force walked in. Allen had washed himself, his dark hair was slicked back, and he wore a sleek, black tunic that made him look much more sophisticated than his usual, flour-covered attire. Even his shoes were shiny, and he was sporting a white rose pinned to the chest of his shirt.

At his arrival, every conversation in the room went silent as gazes swept between Vicky and Allen and back again.

"Vicky, can I have a word with you in private?" he asked, his voice echoing in the now-silent space.

"Absolutely not," Vicky said, glaring at him. "I told you. We're done, Allen."

Immediately, some of the confidence went out of Allen's chest. "Oh, come on, Vicky. Just let me talk to you for five minutes—"

"No. Go home." She folded her arms across her chest and lifted her gaze away from him. "I don't want to see you again."

"Kind of hard, considering we live in the same town," Allen began, but a quick shake of Bev's head quieted *that* dangerous train of thought. "Look, I'm sorry I didn't tell you where I was going, but I promise, if you'll come with me..."

"I'm not going anywhere with you, Allen," Vicky said, standing as her voice grew louder. "You had your chance, and you blew it."

"Just because I didn't tell you where I was going?" he scoffed. "I'm allowed to leave the town,

Vicky—"

"Not for *days*, Allen! I hadn't a clue where you were, if you were dead, in trouble, arrested—"

"Arrested! For what?"

"Who knows? I could think of a lot of different scenarios without any information."

"Well, that's silly," Allen said. "I was *fine*. And I'll tell you everything, but you have to come with me—"

"I told you, I'm not going anywhere with you."

"Damn it, woman, I'm trying to propose if you'll stop being so damn pigheaded!"

The inn went silent once more. Even Bev was taken by surprise by the admission, which, based on Allen's expression, the young baker hadn't intended to make public. His face had gone beet red as he played with the hem of his tunic, seemingly looking for an exit or a way he could melt into the floor.

"You're trying to…what?" Vicky asked, her voice barely above a whisper.

"You heard me." He rubbed the back of his neck. "And I don't *really* fancy an audience, so—"

"Tough." Vicky sniffed, crossing her arms over her chest. "If you want to marry me, you need to ask in front of everyone."

He swallowed hard as he took in the interested faces staring back at him. Bev counted seven, including herself, Earl, Etheldra, Bardoff, and the grannies. Etheldra wore a look of superiority, and

Earl and Bardoff looked like proud fathers as they waited.

"Everyone?"

"Everyone."

"Yes, go on, dearie," Gladys said.

"We're all waiting," Janet said.

Rita sat back. "Make it good."

Allen turned to Bev for help, but she shook her head. He was on his own on this one, and Vicky had a point. If he wanted to marry her, he needed to ask properly.

"Oh, hold on a second." Bev held up her hands. "Ida won't want to miss this. Stay right there."

Allen let out a frustrated sigh as Bev opened the front door. Ida was already standing in the front of her dark shop, perhaps having heard the commotion from all the way in the back.

"Is he doing it?" she asked Bev.

Bev nodded and waved her over. Ida tossed down her apron and dashed across the street in three strides.

"Okay, okay, I'm here," Ida said, smoothing down her shirt. "Oh, Allen, don't you look dashing!"

"I *really* didn't want…" Allen let out a breath. "Never mind." He puffed out his chest and took two steps toward Vicky before dropping to one knee. Ida let out a sob and clung to Bev's hand. "Victoria Hamblin, will you make me the happiest man in Pigsend and marry me?"

Vicky cleared her throat. "More."

"What?" Allen blanched. "What do you mean, *more*?"

"Tell me why you want to marry me." She no longer sounded mad or even coy. There was a serious look on her face, as if she were hanging on Allen's every word.

"Because you infuriate me," he said. "And drive me crazy with your demands. But when I think about a life that doesn't include you..." He shook his head. "It's not really worth living. You're the brightest thing in my world, Vicky, and I'd be a fool if I didn't make you mine."

He reached into his pocket and pulled out a small box. Inside was a golden ring, beset with...

"The bauble!" Bev gasped then covered her mouth as Ida shushed her.

Allen's magical bauble, vibrant green and alive, shimmered as it waited for Vicky's answer.

"Oh, Allen," she whispered, her eyes filling with tears. "Of course I'll be yours!"

She dove into his arms, and for a moment, they were a tangle of laughter, tears, and the awkward putting-on-of-the-ring. But even Bev couldn't help wiping away a tear as Ida bawled openly beside her.

"How in the world did you afford this?" Vicky said, looking down at the bauble. "This is an emerald, isn't it?"

"I—uh…" Allen caught Bev's gaze, and she grinned. "Family heirloom. That's why I was gone. Had to go find a special jeweler to get it put on the ring. Had to find the damn guy first and that took three days longer than I'd anticipated." He shook his head. "I'm sorry I didn't tell you where I was going, but I feared if I said anything, I might spill all the beans. And I wanted this to be perfect for you." He clasped her hand and gazed into her eyes seriously. "It won't ever happen again."

"Too right it won't!" Janet said.

"Congratulations to the happy couple!" Gladys said, jumping up from the table. "We need a toast!"

Rita slapped the table. "Agreed! Your finest vintage, Bev."

"Not sure I have anything like that, but—"

"I picked something up," Allen said. "Just uh… it's at the bakery. One minute." He leaned in to kiss Vicky. "Be right back."

He dashed toward the door, and Vicky squealed as she showed off the ring to Apolinary, who seemed just as excited about it. The grannies oohed and aahed over it as well, but seemed to keep their distance. Could they tell what was in it?

And would this ring set off the shifter again?

"Here!" Allen was back with a bottle of wine. "Not sure there's enough to go around, but—"

"We'll make do," Rita said. "Bev, where are your best glasses?"

Bev pointed the grannies in the right direction as she sidled up to Allen, who was working on getting the cork out of the bottle.

"Three days, eh?" Bev asked.

"I'm sorry I didn't tell you," he said. "Can you forgive me?"

"If Vicky can, I suppose I can, too." She nodded to the marble-like gemstone. "It looks a little smaller than I remember."

"Kind of." Allen lowered his voice. "I met with the barus again."

"Allen!"

"Ssh." He glanced around to make sure no one had heard her. "I'd taken it to a regular jeweler, but they said it was too big to put onto a ring. So I had to find the barus again to ask how I could get it small enough to fit a ring. He said it was the first time someone had asked him to *remove* magic. But he did it." Allen coughed. "Cost me more than a month's salary to get it, but Vicky's worth it."

"Did you find him in the dark forest?" Bev asked.

"No, he wasn't there. That's what took me so long. I had to go looking for him." He cleared his throat. "Had some near-misses with that Dag Flanigan fellow. He's skulking about, looking for some kind of..." He swallowed. "You don't think he's looking for the same thing you are, do you? This...whatever's destroying things in town?"

"Let's hope not," Bev said as the grannies reemerged with the glasses and began divvying up Allen's bottle of wine. Everyone took a glass and raised it.

"To the happy couple," Rita said.

"To the happy—"

ROOOOOOOOOAR!

The whole room shook as a deafening sound echoed from outside. Glasses landed on the table as the whole crowd dashed outside to see what could've caused that noise.

Bev's heart stopped as a large shadow shot toward the sky. The moonlight illuminated unfurling wings and a long, whipping tail as it flew higher in the sky.

"Is that a…"

But as soon as it appeared, the monster shrank in size, disappearing into the night. If Bev squinted, she could almost make out a small shadow falling back down to earth—toward the dark forest.

"Bev?" Allen said.

"I'm on it." She put her fingers to her lips and whistled. "Biscuit?"

The laelaps appeared in the doorway, nose twitching and tail wagging.

"Let's go."

With her trusty glowing stick, Bev and Biscuit ran through the otherwise quiet town toward the north, where the dark forest waited. She didn't fancy running through it in the dark—or in the daytime, either—but this was her one chance to find out what in the world was going on.

Voices echoed from the dark forest ahead, but there was a single shadowy figure in the moonlight. Bev held up her glowing stick as Biscuit growled at her feet. Taking a deep breath, she slowly approached.

The figure heard her, straightened, and spun around. "Who's there?"

Bev almost fell over. "R-Rita?"

The red-haired granny emerged from the darkness, her face void of its usual cheery smile. In fact, she looked almost evil with the shadows covering part of her face. Bev gripped the glowing stick and kept close to Biscuit, who had a thin ridge of hair down his back as he let out a nervous growl.

"What are you doing out here, Bev?" Rita asked, some of her cheer coming back—but it sounded forced.

"I could say the same for you," Bev said. "Where's your sister and cousin?"

"Right here." Gladys and Janet appeared behind Bev, almost out of nowhere. They, too, looked much more sinister in the darkness.

"Quite late for you to be out and about," Janet said.

"You should go back to the inn where it's safe,"

Gladys said.

"I could say the same for you," Bev said. "I'm here because we all heard and saw a giant creature out this way. And I was following it so I could find out who it is."

"It's none of your business," Janet said. "You should go back to town."

"Leave this to us."

"Why? What do you have to do with it?" Bev asked. "You know something, don't you? Are you the ones causing all the problems?"

The three shared a look of surprise before turning to Bev.

"Heavens, no," Rita said.

Janet nodded. "In fact, we were hoping *you* could tell *us* who it is."

"Why?" Bev asked.

"Because we're dragon shifters, too," Gladys said, her expression shifting into one of concern. "And we want to help them."

Chapter Nineteen

"You're…what?"

Of all the creatures Bev had thought might be responsible, *dragon* wasn't on the list. Perhaps a beast of some kind, maybe a wolf or large bear. But dragon…well, that certainly put things into a much different category.

"Dragon shifters, dearie," Rita said.

"What in the world is that?" Bev asked. "You three don't… Well, you don't look like dragons."

"So kind of you to say," Gladys said.

"We're not dragons *all the time*," Janet explained.

Rita nodded. "Just some of the time."

"When we need to stretch the wings a bit," Janet

said.

Bev was having a hard time imagining what that might look like, but put it aside. "So you think whatever's happening in town… That it's a—what did you call it, shifter? Like you?"

They nodded solemnly. "Quite sure," Rita said.

"It's why we came into town," Janet said. "We felt the pull of someone about to take their first shift."

"Good thing we got here when we did," Gladys said.

"Is it always this destructive?" Bev asked.

"Well, usually, we find out who it is and can guide them away from any buildings," Janet said.

"But we're still trying to pinpoint our new shifter friend," Rita said.

"Really?" Bev frowned. "You don't know either?"

Rita gestured to the sky. "Typically, we can sense the magical aura of a shifter—especially when they're this close to a full-fledged transformation."

Gladys shivered. "But this town is practically brimming with magic, so we haven't been able to narrow it down much."

"There's a magical river flowing underground," Bev said. "Runs right by Alice's place, as a matter of fact." She paused. "What do you mean a full-fledged transformation? Didn't we just see one?"

Rita chuckled. "That was merely a preview."

"A real dragon is three times that size," Janet said, almost like it was nothing.

"What we saw was a half shift. Probably a human body with dragon wings." Gladys chuckled. "Can be a bit frightening the first time you see it."

Bev swallowed, glad she hadn't seen *that* sight up close.

"A dragon coming into their own happens in fits and starts. You breathe fire one day, the next you sprout giant wings. It's only for a split second, you see, then it goes away. But eventually..." Janet sighed, looking up at the moon. "You change into your final form. And it's best if you're around other dragons when you do so they can keep a handle on you."

"Then what?" Bev asked.

"Then we'll give them instructions on how to keep themselves and the rest of the town safe, and head off on our merry little way," Rita said.

"Looking for our next shifter," Gladys finished.

Bev watched the three of them, their odd behavior finally making sense. "Is this some sort of...well, I don't know if I'd call it a job, but—"

"Used to be," Rita said, a little sadly. "But now we're the only three dragon shifters left of the official guild."

"There used to be thousands of us." Janet scowled. "That is, until *Her Majesty* came into power."

Bev had heard that before. "But I thought the queen had dragons guarding her castle?"

"Indeed. The queen likes dragons plenty. But dragon *shifters*?" Rita sniffed. "Those are a bit too dangerous for her liking."

"Didn't like how we could hide in plain sight, you know," Gladys said. "We could be sitting at her table then transform into a monster capable of eating her."

Seeing the destruction in town, Bev had a rare moment of agreement with the queen.

"Now it's up to us to carry on the knowledge," Gladys said. "And find as many others as we can scattered throughout the countryside."

"*Especially* since dragon shifters are all but outlawed in these parts," Rita said. "We have to be careful of the queen's soldiers. They'll waste no time taking us away in handcuffs if they think we might possibly change."

"Can't you turn into a dragon and eat them?" Bev asked.

"They place potent anti-magic amulets on us," Janet said. "We use them, too, especially with newly transitioned shifters to keep their magic at bay. But that's after they get their first shift out of the way."

"Based on the timing of these incidents, we're getting close to the full shift," Gladys said. "I don't suppose you have an idea who it might be, do you?"

"I have theories," Bev paused. "Though I'm not

sure I know what I'm looking for anymore. Would someone become a shifter through their parents?"

"Bloodlines do play into it." Janet nodded. "Obviously, we're related."

"But with most of the stronger lines wiped out, we're left to find flukes and abnormalities," Rita said. "Once upon a time, the Guild would've ignored such an abnormality, but…well, we can't afford not to seek them out."

Gladys smiled. "Any shifter's better than nothing."

Bev couldn't imagine what a powerful dragon might look like—and hoped she never did. "So there's no telling who it could be?"

"It manifests sometime in early adulthood," Gladys said. "We've been keeping a close eye on the youngsters in town. Especially ones who've been close to the concentrations of magic."

"And there's been plenty of that going around," Bev said. "We can safely rule out everyone who was at the town meeting. The scones were covered in magic."

"Oh, we knew," Gladys said, with a sparkle in her eye. "Very clever, that."

"If we hadn't been afraid we'd be triggered into our own transformation, we'd have eaten the lot," Rita said.

"Who wasn't at the town meeting?" Janet asked.

"Allen Mackey and his girlfriend—*fiancée*—

Vicky Hamblin," Bev said. "But I was standing right next to them just now."

"Mackey, the baker?" Rita asked. Bev nodded. "We investigated him but found his magic to be the wrong kind."

"His mother was a pobyd," Bev explained. "But Allen doesn't use magic in his confections these days. That ring he gave Vicky was all that he had left of his mother's magic."

"It seemed a bit different," Rita said.

"Nobody else was missing from the town meeting?" Gladys asked.

Bev shook her head then stopped. "How young is young adulthood? Could it be one of the local kids? None of them were at the town meeting.

"It very well could be. We've been trailing Bardoff around town, hoping we might see something from one of them," Janet said.

That certainly explained why they seemed to be everywhere the kids were. "Vicky's brother and his two friends were near Earl's backyard," Bev said. "He thought they were sneaking into his workshop to drink his spirits. If they accidentally handled the mayor's potent magical resin—" She stopped. "Grant had two of my magical scones."

"Well, that certainly could've caused something to happen," Gladys said.

"Can you tell us anything about the siblings?" Rita asked.

"I don't know much about them, other than that their mother died several years ago and their father left them in a lurch," Bev said. "His two friends, Valta and PJ, are always with him. Maybe they've seen something they want to share."

"We've tried talking with them, but they don't seem too friendly," Janet said.

"There's more than one way to lay an egg," Gladys said.

Bev started. "Do you…lay eggs?"

"Oh, don't be silly," Rita said, waving her hand.

"I'll see what I can find out," Bev said. "How much time do we have before they…well… transform for real?"

The three shared a look, silently conversing with one another. "Days at this rate," Janet said.

"Maybe less." Gladys tutted.

Rita nodded. "If they're already taking shape, even for a moment, then we're getting close to the full thing."

"What if that happens before we get to them?" Bev asked.

"Then there's a chance the whole town could burn down, or be stomped flat, or people could… well…" Gladys gestured toward the town.

Rita finished for her. "Get eaten."

"Right. Let's avoid that," Bev said. "Why don't I take another crack at the kids? I'm friendly with their parents and guardians. Maybe there's something new they want to share." She wasn't optimistic, but at least she knew what she was dealing with. "Especially if I let them know you're here to help."

"Oh, don't mention us until you're sure," Rita said.

Janet nodded. "Must keep a low profile."

Bev hardly thought that they'd kept a *low* profile during their stay in Pigsend. "Fine, I'll make sure I know who it is before I reveal you. But at least if they know *someone's* in town to help, maybe they'll be more eager to share information."

"We'll stay as long as it takes," Gladys said. "Every shifter reveals themselves eventually."

"Unless we get wind of a queen's soldier." Rita pursed her lips. "Then we must leave."

Bev stopped. "Really? Just like that? Even if we don't know who's transforming?"

"We can't jeopardize our own safety," Janet said. "We're all that remains of the dragon shifters in this world."

"If we're captured, there'd be no one to help the next shifter who needs it," Rita said. "And that is a fate that cannot be allowed to happen."

The grannies wanted to keep searching the countryside for the shifter, promising Bev that they were perfectly capable of finding their way back to the inn and were more equipped to search the dark fields and towns than Bev was.

In the darkness, Bev lay awake, staring at the ceiling and trying to imagine what it must be like for the poor soul who was transforming into a giant dragon. Her heart softened toward Grant, who'd been nothing but rude and cagey to her for at least a week. Was he simply hiding all his stress about the mysterious happenings?

Unfortunately, the Hamblin siblings had moved back into their newly rebuilt apartment the night before, so Bev had to wait to ask them about where Grant might've been. Allen hadn't been much help, telling Bev that he and Vicky had celebrated late into the night as he dropped off a basket of peach preserve pastries.

Mid-afternoon, Bev and Biscuit took a walk down the street to the seamstress shop. Earl was there painting the outside a bright white, and to Bev's surprise, Grant and Valta were helping.

"That's right, easy brush strokes," Earl said, standing behind them. "Nice work."

"Getting into a new profession?" Bev asked.

"Well, my usual helpers seem to have disappeared this morning, and these kids seemed keen to help," he said, looking around. "Have you seen the gran—er, those marvelous ladies?"

"I think they're out for a walk," Bev said, hoping the lie was believable. "They'll probably show up once they see you're back at work. You know how they are."

"Indeed, I do. Wouldn't be surprised if they were halfway to Middleburg!"

"Really?" Bev frowned. "Why?"

"Getting more wood," Earl said, a little curiously. "And in the meantime, I've got these two strapping young folks who said they were eager to help me finish the job." He slapped Grant on the shoulder.

"Good to hear," Bev said. "Is Vicky inside?"

"Yep." Grant dipped his brush back in the can. "Why?"

"Just wanted to…congratulate her," Bev said, walking by him as he glared at her. "We didn't get a chance to talk last night before that thing showed up. Whatever it was."

"Yeah, it was something, wasn't it? Saw you go running after it," Earl said. "Did you find it?"

Bev shook her head. "Disappeared into the sky."

He pushed back his cap and whistled. "Looked awfully big. Where do you think it came from?"

"Haven't a clue," Bev said, walking toward the front door. "Did you happen to see anything, kids?"

Valta took her brush to the walls. "I was home in bed."

"Same." Grant stepped beside her to paint.

Bev started. He certainly hadn't been home because his home was still under construction. But he ignored her, so Bev didn't press, walking by them and into the shop.

Inside smelled of sawdust and fresh paint as Apolinary worked on a dress hanging on a mannequin and Vicky sat sewing, her ring glinting in the morning light. But the newly engaged seamstress seemed anything but overjoyed.

"I've got this giant, beautiful ring, and all anyone can talk about is that stupid monster," she whined as Apolinary shook her head. "The Brewer twins barely eked out a congratulations before bringing it up. Hey, Bev."

"Morning, ladies," Bev said, walking up to the counter. "Sorry to hear your big night was overshadowed."

"Besides that, what does it matter if you get congratulations or not? You're engaged, isn't that what matters?" Apolinary huffed. "I've got to get the rest of the fabric off the wagon. Do you think the paint's dry in here? Don't want to risk it getting all over everything."

"Seems fine to me," Vicky said, adjusting her ring again.

Apolinary waited, seeming to want Vicky to help her, but the other woman kept gazing at her new jewelry. After a moment, she scoffed and disappeared out the door.

"Vicky, you should probably pull your head out of the clouds, or you might find yourself out of a job," Bev said with a chuckle.

Beasts and Baking

She tutted, putting down the tunic. "What can I do for you, Bev?"

Out the window, Grant was getting chastised by Earl for his too-fast brush strokes.

"What in the world are they doing with Earl?" Bev asked.

"Oh. This morning, the two of them showed up and asked Earl if they could help." She shrugged. "Guess Bardoff gave them the day off school. Or maybe that giant monster scared them into wanting to help out for a change instead of cutting up."

Or maybe they're feeling guilty because one of them did it. "Well, good for them. I'm glad they've gotten some good direction."

"Well?" Vicky prompted. "What can I do for you?"

Bev wasn't ready to leave the conversation, so she turned to the one topic Vicky wouldn't mind talking about. "When's the wedding?"

"I don't think it'll be too far off," Vicky said, standing. "I'm sure my *mother's* family will want to come. Not that they've given us one lick of help since she died, but—"

"Where are they from?" Bev asked. Of course, she didn't think Vicky would outright say her family were a pack of dragon shifters, but any clue would be helpful.

"Sheepsburg," Vicky said. "I've got two stuffy aunts and an insufferable uncle. They never forgave my mother for marrying a farmhand, so I never hear from them." She smiled, with a little sneer. "You'd better believe they're going to be invited, though. Show them what we've been doing here in Pigsend."

"Your father was from here, then?" Bev asked. "Why did he fight in the war?"

"Don't believe anyone had much of a choice," Vicky said. "But for him, it was the money. Of course, if he'd done the honorable thing and died, we might've gotten a few silvers from the queen every month."

Bev nodded. "Do you know what he did in the king's army?"

"Foot soldier, I reckon," she said. "Why so interested?"

"Just curious." Bev pushed a scrap of fabric along the counter. "Lots of folks fought for different reasons, I hear. Didn't know if he had a vested interest or—"

"That's right." She smiled as she put the last bolt on the table. "You don't remember anything before the war, do you?"

Bev shook her head.

"He went because the king was offering money," Vicky said. "Nothing more, nothing less."

Bev didn't know Vicky well enough to ask her whether she was hiding some magical ability. But she did notice the green bauble on her finger. "Did Allen tell you where he got that?"

She looked at the ring and smiled warmly. "Not really. He said it's very precious to him."

"It is," Bev said. "Just… Just be careful. I know it would kill him if anything happened to it."

"Why in the world would you say that?" Vicky asked, frowning. "Is there something you want to tell me?"

Bev sighed, hearing Grant getting another earful from Earl. "Nothing. Let me know when you have a date, and I'll be sure to clear the books at the inn."

"That was absolutely pointless," Bev said to Biscuit as they walked back to the inn. "And a few hours wasted. Good thing we didn't get another big dragon swooping over town."

He stopped, his nose twitching and the hair on his back rising.

"What is it?" Bev asked, as she opened the front door. Once inside, she stopped short.

"Well, Bev," Dag Flanigan said. "So good to see you again."

Chapter Twenty

"Well, hello," Bev said, after a moment of panic. "Mr. Flanigan. Welcome back."

Although there had been a spate of queen's soldiers in town of late, none of them had made a repeat visit—until now. Karolina Hunter had been all but run out of town, and Claude seemed to be frequenting Harvest Festivals and the like. But it seemed Mr. Flanigan was the first amongst them to make a repeat visit.

"Likewise." He leaned on the counter, the gnarly scar on his face somewhat off-putting. "Any more trouble happening in town?"

"Not so much," Bev said as she quickly crossed the room to the front counter.

"Really? Because I hear you've had a spate of buildings being demolished."

"Oh, right." She laughed nervously. "Well, that. But no more blackmailers."

"I'm not here for blackmailers. I'm hunting magic." He inhaled deeply. "And this place is *covered* with it."

Bev forced a smile. She'd seen firsthand what a magic-hunter like Flanigan was capable of and didn't want him sniffing around the inn too much. She'd have to dispose of Etheldra's magical tea as soon as she got back into the kitchen.

"So." He surveyed her. "Any idea what's causing the trouble in town? You're always the one embroiled in these things."

"Wish I could say," Bev said, hoping she sounded honest. "Do you have any idea what it could be?"

"Some theories. I've been hearing about dragon shifters." He paused. "Heard anything about that?"

Bev could've sworn he could read her mind—but she did her best to keep her tone neutral. "Dragon shifters? That's a bit out of my depth, I have to say. Can't say I've seen any dragons around these parts."

"Then what about that shadow last night?" he said. "I have several witnesses say you took off looking for it."

"Witnesses?"

He nodded. "Been chatting with the baker and his girl."

"Fiancée," Bev said. "Just got engaged last night. What else did Allen say?"

"The baker didn't say a thing," he said with a look. "His fiancée, however, was quite chatty. Told me you went off searching for the shadow."

"I did," Bev said. "Didn't find it. But I didn't venture into the dark forest. Not really my favorite place—even in daylight."

He let out a long breath before reaching into his pocket. Bev held her breath, half-expecting him to pull out a pair of handcuffs, but he slammed two gold coins onto the counter.

"One night."

"Just you, then?" Bev asked.

"Just me." He cracked a grin. "The rest of my troops are encamped near the dark forest, actually. Surprised you didn't run into them."

And thank goodness whoever the shifter is didn't either.

"Like I said, I try to steer clear of the place." She slid one gold coin toward him. "Just one gold for the night."

"Keep it," he said. "In case you remember anything that might be pertinent."

"I'm sure I won't," Bev said, pushing the coin back. "Memory isn't my strong suit, if you hadn't heard."

Beasts and Baking

"Yes, I did a little digging on you, Bev-the-innkeeper," Dag said. "Interesting past you have."

Bev started. "You… You know about my past?"

He could say anything he wanted, and Bev wouldn't be able to discern truth from fiction. The only thing she had were flashes, and one of those flashes had her at the same battle where Mr. Flanigan had earned his gnarly scar. And from Bev's limited understanding, she'd been on the opposing side.

"I think I know as much as you do," Flanigan said, stepping back from the counter. "Had a chat with Karolina Hunter and Renault Lank—you knew him as Claude, I believe. Both of them said you were *highly* suspicious. Renault had his doubts that you even suffer from memory loss, perhaps on the run from something—or someone."

"Well, if they have any clues you'd like to share," Bev said. "I'm all ears."

She waited, and the silence stretched out between them.

"Hm." He stepped back. "Which room am I in?"

"Oh, um." She checked the log book, her gaze scanning over the grannies' names, and her stomach dropped. Would they be leaving? What did that mean for the town? What if—

"Ms. Bev?"

"Room five," Bev said, grabbing the key and

pushing it across the counter before she gave him more reason to be suspicious. "And dinner will be ready at six. Believe I'll be making some pork loin today." Not that she'd purchased meat or done anything other than get her bread proofing.

"Along with that rosemary bread, hm?" He cracked a surly smile. "Can't say that wasn't a big reason for me to come back in town, either. Left something of a craving on my tongue."

"Won me second place at the Harvest Festival," Bev said, nodding to the ribbon. "Not sure if Claude—Renault, I suppose—heard about that. But it was quite a feather in my cap. First time I'd entered the contest, and to win second place?" She was almost babbling now, but she was rather proud of that ribbon, after all.

"Mm." He snatched the key off the counter. "I'll see you at six, Ms. Bev."

"Just Bev," she muttered as he ascended the stairs.

Once the door shut, Bev turned and rushed out of the inn.

Bev hoped, perhaps, that the grannies had found the shifter and were already on their merry way. But her hopes sank when she found them at the schoolhouse, discussing plans for rebuilding with Earl and Bardoff.

"Left the kids in charge of finishing the paint

job," Earl said as Bev joined their group. "Assume Apolinary would skin them alive if they messed things up."

"Probably," Bev said with a tense smile. "Can I speak with you ladies a moment?"

The grannies followed Bev until they were a safe distance away.

"You look like someone's canceled your birthday," Gladys said.

"What's wrong?" Rita asked.

"Dag Flanigan showed up at my inn," Bev said, her voice low. "Are you familiar with him?"

Based on the way their expressions darkened, they were.

"Where is he?" Janet nodded toward the other side of town. "At the inn?"

"Yeah. He was upstairs when I left, but I don't think he'll stay there long," Bev said. "Please tell me you found who you were looking for last night?"

"Unfortunately, no," Janet said.

"Did you get a chance to speak with the kids?" Bev asked.

"They're about as chatty as a steel trap," Rita said. "Definitely hiding something. We can't help them if they don't open up to us first."

"And even if they had," Janet said with a sad shake of her head, "if Flanigan is in town, it seems our time in Pigsend has come to an end."

"But, cousin," Gladys started, earning her a

shake of the head from Rita.

"We can't risk it," Rita said, sounding awfully sad to admit it. "We must be on our way."

"Can't share a building with the man who'd have us wiped off the map," Janet said. "We're so sorry, Bev."

"What happens when the shifter...well, shifts?" Bev asked. "Who'll be here to control them?"

"Flanigan." Rita's face was clear about one thing: Flanigan's methods wouldn't involve containment. Just elimination.

"I wish we could've had more time," Janet said. "Truly. It breaks our hearts to have to leave you so quickly."

Bev licked her lips. "Is it possible for you to leave without...leaving? Maybe give me one more night to find out who it is?"

The grannies shared a look of indecision, but their answer was cut short.

"Is this one of the destroyed buildings?"

Flanigan strolled up, his queenspin shiny on his chest as he inspected the property. In the daylight, he was even more formidable, and that scar seemed to reflect the light. Bardoff nodded to him with a tight smile and Earl averted his gaze, but the grannies plastered on their usual cheery expressions. If Bev hadn't just been talking with them about leaving in a hurry, she wouldn't have guessed a thing was amiss.

"What was this?" Flanigan asked.

"A schoolhouse," Bardoff said.

The soldier knelt to inspect the splintered wood on the ground. "When did it happen?"

"Two nights ago," Earl said. "While we were all in a town meeting."

"Oh?" He rose, spying the grannies. "Who are you? And why are you loitering?"

"I'm Rita, this is my sister Janet, and our cousin Gladys," she said with a smile that Bev knew she certainly didn't mean. "We're guests at the inn."

"Darn glad they are, too!" Earl said, perhaps feeling the need to come to their aid. "They've been helping me rebuild."

"Rather hard work for ladies your age, isn't it?" Flanigan asked, narrowing his gaze as Bev's pulse spiked.

"We get by," Rita said.

"Happy to help these delightful people," Gladys said.

"Is that *Dag Flanigan*?"

Hendry seemed to have heard the conversation from clear across the town square and through the closed doors of the town hall, because she breezed over with a smile on her face. Bev couldn't help but notice the particular shade of purple of her tunic.

"I'm *so* sorry to have missed you the first time you were in town," she said, extending her hand. "Jo Hendry. The mayor of this magnificent town."

"Pleasure." Though from his tone, it wasn't. "What can you tell me about this destruction?"

"Oh, well, it's been a few places here and there," Hendry said. "Earl's workshop was the first one, but we're pretty sure it was a rambunctious group of teenagers. Aren't we, Bev?"

"Can't say—"

"Alice's barn, well… I'm pretty sure there was a nasty storm that had blown through," Hendry said. "As far as the seamstress's shop, I'm not quite sure what to make of that one. Or the schoolhouse. Near everyone in town was attending a town meeting when it happened."

"And the large shadow last night?" Flanigan asked.

"Your guess is as good as mine," Hendry said, brushing the front of her tunic. "But I suppose that's why you've come to town, isn't it?"

"It is." He glanced behind her toward the town hall. "Rustin around?"

"Our dear sheriff is taking a much-needed vacation," she said. "We do expect him back any day now. And not a moment too soon, what with all the *curiosities* happening in town."

"Well," Flanigan spun around to make sure *everyone* in the vicinity knew he was talking to them, "if any of you should remember anything you saw last night, or anything related to these *curiosities,* you should report them to me. We're officially taking over the investigation in town."

"What do you think it is?" Bardoff asked.

"Can't say for sure," Flanigan said. "But to me, it appears to be a dragon shifter."

"Oh my!" Gladys said, putting her hand over her heart.

Janet gasped. "A shifter?"

"What in the world is that?" Rita asked.

"A person who can destroy the town if they get a mind to," Flanigan said. "Trust me when I say you'll want to tell me who it is before they completely change. Don't think this quaint little town would survive a full dragon stomping around in it."

Bardoff looked concerned, as did Earl. The grannies were quite good at acting surprised. Hendry was mildly interested. Flanigan scrutinized each of their faces before deciding they weren't worth bothering further.

"Keep that in mind," he said, turning on his heel, "while you think about who you're protecting." He paused. "Innkeeper, didn't you say something about dinner?"

"I did," Bev said, weakly. "Suppose I should get on it."

"We'll see you at six, then?" Rita asked.

"Yes, of course," Bev said, knowing that the grannies would be long gone. "At six."

Bev walked away from the schoolhouse with

every intention of going to the butchers and putting in that pork loin order. But instead, she found herself walking back toward the seamstress shop. The grannies might've been leaving town, but if Bev found the culprit, she'd be able to send that person to safety along with them.

She just had to find them.

Vicky was the only one working, though she seemed to have put more of the fabric away. The outside had been completely painted, and the kids were nowhere to be found.

"Back again?" Vicky asked, a little thinly. "What can I do for you now, Bev?"

"Where's your brother?"

She started, putting down the tunic. "Why?"

"Because I think he's in trouble, and I need to find him before…someone else does," Bev said.

Vicky rose, crossing the room with her brow furrowed. "What in the world has he gotten himself into now?"

"I don't think he's done it intentionally."

She scoffed. "You still think he's behind all this destruction, don't you? Doesn't matter how much I vouch for his whereabouts."

She chewed her lip. "I think he might be turning into something else. Unbeknownst to him. Maybe his friends know. But—"

"That's the most ridiculous thing I've ever heard," Vicky snapped.

"It's not." Grant walked into the front room, his face an ashen color. Behind him, Valta followed, her lips pressed together in a thin line.

"Grant?" Vicky said. "You aren't… Tell me you aren't the one behind this."

He glanced between Vicky and Bev then back to Valta, who seemed as indecisive as he was.

"It's PJ, isn't it?" Bev asked softly.

He didn't say anything for a long pause, then gave one curt nod. "And what of it?" Grant asked. "Are you going to turn them in to that Flanigan guy?"

"No," Bev said, glancing out the front window to make sure said guy wasn't standing there eavesdropping. "If you tell me what you know, there's a chance I can get him to safety with friends. But only if we act quickly. Otherwise, he might be leaving town in handcuffs with Dag Flanigan."

"There's no need," Valta said. "He's long gone."

"Which way did he go?" Bev asked.

"We're not saying," Grant replied. "He's left town, and that's the end of it."

"That's not the end of it, though," Bev said. "Sometime in the next day—maybe even today—PJ is going to have his full shift. And whoever he's with is going to be dealing with a mindless dragon instead of—"

"Dragon?" Valta squeaked, covering her mouth. "Grant, we—"

"Hush, Valta," he snapped. "We made a promise."

"I know where they went," Vicky said softly. "Apolinary left about an hour ago with her sister and brother-in-law—the Norrises," Vicky said, not taking her eyes off Grant. "Thought it was strange timing, considering we just got the shop back up. She told me her mother had taken ill and they were going to check on her, but I didn't see a letter or anything like that." She paused. "They said they were headed toward Sheepsburg."

After a long pause, Grant nodded.

"Thank you," Bev said. They had a head start, but she might be able to catch up with them if she left now. "And if either of you see Flanigan—"

"I'll be sure to send him the other way," Grant said. "He won't get PJ if I have anything to say about it."

"Yeah," Valta said, puffing out her chest.

"Just be careful," Bev said, hurrying to the door.

Chapter Twenty-One

"Biscuit, I need you to find PJ," Bev said, kneeling down to her laelaps. "Do you know who I'm talking about?"

Biscuit retracted his tongue, giving her an odd look with his lip curled up, then turned and darted down the street. Dusk was falling, and there would be hungry folks at the inn looking for dinner, but this was far more important. She'd stopped at the inn long enough to grab Biscuit and her glowing stick then headed east.

Her laelaps had a white spot on the tip of his tail, which was visible even as the light dwindled around her. Bev didn't know if Apolinary and the Norrises had taken a horse or a wagon or gone on foot, but with an hour head start, they were pretty far down the road.

Biscuit's gait went from a trot to an all-out gallop, and Bev could only just keep up. In the distance, figures huddled on the side of the road and her heart sank. Had Flanigan already found them?

But as she came closer, someone moaned in pain, and a new fear came over her. Was the dragon about to take shape?

"Go get the grannies, Biscuit," Bev said. "I don't know where they've gone off to, but—"

The laelaps didn't need to be told twice and scampered back toward town. Bev hoped he would be fast enough to find them before PJ shifted.

"PJ?" Bev called, holding the glowing stick aloft.

The light from the glowing mushrooms illuminated Apolinary, Holly, and Pip, who were blocking the fourth person. The three adults turned to Bev as if she were a snake, and she took a step back from their ferocity.

"Be on your way, Bev," Pip snarled.

"This is none of your business," Holly said, turning back to her son.

"It is, because I know what's happening to him," she said, coming closer. "I promise, I mean you no harm."

"What's happening to him?" Holly asked, her voice quiet as she brushed his forehead.

The poor teenager was as ashen as the dead grass

he lay in, sweaty and pale as he clutched his stomach. Bev wished she'd thought ahead to bring him some mint, but something told her that wouldn't do much to stave off the inevitable.

Before she could say a word, there was movement in the fields beyond. Bev put her finger to her mouth and rose.

Out of the darkness, no fewer than six soldiers appeared—led by Dag Flanigan.

"What in the world is going on here?" he asked, sounding as if he knew exactly what was happening.

"We were headed to Sheepsburg," Apolinary said, her voice steady. "Our mother's taken ill."

"And so has your boy," Dag said, grinning like a cat that caught a bird. "Seems to be going around, isn't it?"

"He ate something that didn't agree with him," Pip said, sounding much less confident than Apolinary.

"And you, innkeeper," Dag said, turning his attention to Bev. "How fortuitous you're out here. Shouldn't you be back at your inn, making dinner?"

Bev thought quickly. "My dog got loose. Chased him all the way up here, and I came across Pip and Holly."

"Well?" Dag looked around. "Where is he?"

"Told him to go get help," Bev said, cracking a smile. "He's a good listener when he wants to be. Probably ran all the way here to let me know that the Norris boy wasn't doing so well."

PJ let out a whimpering moan as he clutched his stomach. He certainly looked like he'd eaten something that hadn't agreed with him. But as he let out a small belch, a little smoke rose from his lips.

"Besides that, I left the grannies at the inn to tend to the meal," Bev said, praying Flanigan hadn't seen that. "Seeing as they eat most of it anyway—"

"They weren't there, and neither was your dinner," Dag said, taking a step forward. "Your story seems to have plenty of holes in it, *Bev*."

"Oh! *Here* you are!"

"Good thing we caught you!"

"Can't see a darn thing out here."

To Bev's surprise, the grannies emerged from the other side of the fields, chattering and talking as if nothing were wrong. Biscuit was right behind them, his tail up and his golden eyes fixed on Dag Flanigan.

"What are you three doing here?" Dag asked.

"Well, we were on our way back from Middleburg," Janet said.

"Off to get some more wood for the schoolhouse," Rita said.

"We've worn a hole in these roads, I'll tell you that." Gladys nodded.

"When this *lovely* dog came to us and barked," Janet continued. "Well, we assumed he wanted us to come with him."

Rita walked toward the ill teenager. "And here we find poor PJ Norris in need of help."

"And wouldn't you know, we have just the ticket." Gladys reached into her pocket and pulled out several green sprigs.

"Mint! Best thing in the world for indigestion," Janet said.

Under Dag's suspicious glare, Rita knelt beside PJ and helped him eat the sprigs. "There you go. Yes, swallow it all. You'll be right as rain in a moment."

Indeed, from Bev's vantage, the boy's color improved almost instantly.

"Thanks," he croaked—and Bev wasn't so sure a little smoke didn't come out of his mouth.

"There, now. Let's get you up and on your feet," Gladys said, reaching to take the boy's arm. "That's a good lad."

"Brush off this dirt and grass," Janet said, patting him on the back. "Can't be walking around like we've been rolling in the grass."

"Now, shall we head back into town?" Rita asked brightly.

"You three aren't fooling me," Dag said, walking toward them with a menacing sort of stare. "I know you're all dragon shifters, and I know *this* boy is about to turn into a giant monster. It's the reason for all the destruction in town, and if the rumors are true, you three are the most powerful dragons—"

The three grannies burst into twittering laughter. "Oh, Mr. Flanigan, you are quite the comic!" Rita bellowed.

"Dragons? Us?" Janet wiped away tears.

"Oh, dear me, cousin, look at my wings." Gladys put her hands under her armpits and flapped her elbows. "I'm a big dragon!"

"You mock me," Flanigan said.

"Would you take a look at us?" Janet said, gesturing to her and her sisters. "We're here to help the town. And you think we're *dragons*?"

"Dragon *shifters*," Flanigan said through gritted teeth. "And if you aren't, then who is?"

ROOOOOAR!

The sound echoed from the left, *not* from the ill boy, who seemed as perplexed as everyone else. All heads turned toward the east, where a giant fireball flew up into the sky and exploded into multi-colored sparks. A red tinge illuminated the trees, before orange flames reached toward the sky.

"What's going on?" Dag barked at the Norrises as if they were somehow responsible. "What did you do?"

"We didn't do anything," Holly said, blinking wildly. "I—"

Another ear-splitting roar echoed through the valley before a huge, winged shadow floated across the sky.

"The dragon!" Dag cried. "It's shifted! Let's go!"

They didn't need to be told twice, pulling their swords and running after the dragon in the sky, leaving the grannies, Bev, and the Norrises staring in awe.

"There can't be a *second* shifter in town, can there?" Bev said, looking at the grannies.

"Not to our knowledge, but anything is…" Rita squinted. "Wait a second."

Bev followed her gaze. The shadowy figure didn't appear to be flapping its wings but bobbing along on the wind. Had Bev not seen PJ fly the night before, she wouldn't have been able to tell the difference.

"That's not a dragon," Janet said.

"Then what the heck is it?" Holly snapped.

Before anyone could answer, PJ let out a loud groan and clutched his stomach as he swayed. His parents swarmed on him, fretting and fussing at him.

"We have to keep moving," Apolinary said. "Get him out of here."

"Getting him out won't help what's happening," Rita said, rolling up her sleeves.

"Not much will stop it, but we can delay it," Janet said, gently kneeling down next to him.

"Give him here, dearie," Gladys said, gently taking PJ's hand as she reached into her pocket. "Here you go, sweetheart. Have some more mint.

It'll help with the heartburn."

"Who are you?" Holly asked, though her tone had softened as PJ chewed on the green leaves.

"We're here to help," Rita said, patting PJ's hand. "There, is that better?"

"M-much." His color had improved. "What's happening to me?"

"How much do you remember of last night?" Janet asked.

"I remember… Grant gave me a scone," he said, rubbing his head. "Then I woke up at the edge of town."

"I told you to steer clear of him," Pip said. "Nothing but bad news."

"You can't blame Grant for giving PJ a scone covered in magic icing," Rita said. "You can blame Bev for that."

"Hey…" Bev scowled.

"What's happening to our son?" Holly asked. "Please, we're desperate for answers."

"What's your last name, love?" Janet asked.

"Our…what?"

"Your last name?"

"Norris," Pip said.

"Mm. Not you, then." Rita turned to Apolinary and Holly. "And yours?"

"McGraw," they said in unison.

The grannies shared a look. "I think there might've been a McGraw out this way," Janet said.

Gladys shook her head. "No, I think that was a McAlister."

"Maybe a McPhearson?" Rita offered before turning to the adults again. "Any other names in your family?"

"I don't understand," Holly said. "What in the world is going on? Why do you need our names?"

"Your son is a dragon shifter," Rita said matter-of-factly. "He's quite young to be presenting already, so he must be descended from a powerful line. We're trying to pinpoint which family it might be."

"D-dragon?" Holly said.

"You've got to be kidding me," Pip replied.

"I'm not a…" PJ looked at his hands. "You're mad."

"Only a bit, but that's all right," Rita said. "Why don't you tell us what's been happening to you lately? Start with Earl's workshop."

"He was nowhere near the workshop," Pip said.

"Is that true?" Gladys asked.

PJ cleared his throat, looking a little guilty. "Not exactly."

"*Pip Junior!*" Holly cried. "You lied to us!"

"We weren't… I mean, we weren't trying to… We didn't *mean* to burn it down!"

"Tell us what happened," Janet said, a kind smile on her face.

"Valta, Grant, and I… We like to take a nip of Earl's spirits."

"*PJ.*"

"Let him finish," Gladys said, holding up her hand.

"So we took a nip one day then the next thing I knew..." He swallowed. "I let out a huge burp...of fire."

"Yes, that'll do it," Janet said. "What about Alice's barn?"

Holly started, looking at PJ. "You'd gone there to retrieve my knife."

He nodded. "I cut through ol' Bathilda's yard. Saw her weird sheep. Petted them. Then I started to feel funny." He shivered. "Next thing I knew, I'm lying in the rubble of Alice's barn. Got away before she saw me."

"You were in my shop, weren't you?" Apolinary said, coming down off the wagon. "Did you touch any of the fabrics?"

"Grant wanted help moving them," he said, averting his gaze.

"Oh, *PJ.*" Holly shook her head.

"What about the night of the town meeting?" Bev asked.

"Valta stole a couple pastries off the table," he said. "We were eating them behind the schoolhouse when it all went blank again." He paused. "But... they said I'd sprouted...wings."

"I should've stayed home with you," Holly said. "But I knew if I didn't go, Earl would stand up and tell everyone it was PJ's fault. I couldn't risk a mob coming after my boy." She smoothed down his hair. "He's a good kid."

"Of course he is," Janet said. "He can't help that he's got dragon blood in his veins."

"This is insane," Pip said. "Our son isn't a… *dragon*. If he were, why aren't my wife and I?"

"Sometimes it can skip a generation—or three," Rita said. "But somewhere in you or your wife's line, there's a dragon shifter. And your son has manifested it." She paused. "Or will, soon."

"You know we're telling the truth," Janet said gently. "Otherwise, why were you leaving town?"

Holly shared a look with her husband before turning to her son, lip quivering. "We don't know what's going on with our boy."

"Then let us help you," Rita said.

"How?" Holly asked.

"We'll take PJ—" Janet started.

"And you, of course, if you'd like to go," Gladys interjected.

"To a safe place," Rita finished. "Help him through his first full transformation. Keep him from destroying anything else."

"Or hurting anyone," Gladys said.

"Once he's got his powers under control, he'll be free to come back to Pigsend and continue his studies," Janet said. "And we'll move on to find another shifter in need."

Holly seemed ready to argue, but PJ weakly lifted his hand to rest on her arm. "Mom, I want to go with them."

"Are you sure?" Holly took his hand. "What if..."

"It's not like things can get any worse," he said, inching off the wagon. "I'm burping fire and sprouting wings. At least if I go with them...maybe I won't make a mess of things."

"If you're sure..." Holly cupped his face. "I—"

Footsteps approached, and the grannies went stick-straight. Fear dripped down Bev's back. Had there been a soldier nearby listening to the conversation? Was Dag on his way back to finish what he'd started?

"Show yourselves," Janet said, her voice full of ice.

Bev squinted as the bushes nearby rattled.

"C-Grant?" PJ sputtered. "*Valta?*"

The two teenagers emerged from the darkness, the moonlight illuminating their soot-covered faces. They looked sheepish, almost as if they'd been caught sneaking Earl's spirits.

"What are you doing here?" Bev asked. "And what did you do?"

"Got those soldiers off your back," Grant said proudly.. "So you can go off with these grannies and turn into a big honking dragon."

"How did you do that?" Rita asked, with an

approving smile.

"We heard those soldiers planning to catch you," Valta said. "So we put our heads together."

"I used some fabric in the shop to make a dragon-shaped kite," Valta said. "Grant nailed together some wood to make a frame."

"I made the candle," Grant said. "Lit it on fire, just like those sky lanterns Bardoff had us making." He nodded to the dragon floating in the sky. "And there it goes."

"Only had the one big fireball in it, though," Valta said.

"How'd you manage that?" Rita asked.

"Chemical reaction," Grant said. "Wrapped a small ball of cinnamon in burlap and set it on fire. By the time it got high enough in the sky, it exploded."

"We weren't sure what a dragon's fire looks like," Grant said. "I hope it's enough to fool the soldiers."

"By the time he gets back here, we'll be long gone," Rita said. "And by the time your friend gets back, Flanigan won't be able to tell whether he's a shifter or not."

The two teens shared a relieved smile before PJ let out a small belch, and a puff of black smoke came out.

"But we'd probably better hurry," Janet said. "Are you ready, PJ?"

"Be careful," Holly said, squeezing his hand.

"You three should go visit your mother in Sheepsburg," Rita said. "Just in case."

"She'd love to see us," Apolinary replied, tears in her eyes.

PJ gave his family and friends a final hug then followed the grannies into the darkness. Holly let out a small sob before climbing back onto the wagon with Pip. Apolinary clicked her tongue, and the horse moved forward.

Then it was just Bev, Grant, and Valta.

"I must say..." Bev said with a smile. "Floating lantern? Burning cinnamon? Bardoff would be proud his lessons are sinking in."

"Yeah, well, don't tell him," Grant said, rubbing the soot off his face. "Bad enough *you* know."

Bev laughed as they turned back to town. "I think you'll find that I keep a great many secrets. I think I can keep one more from your schoolmaster."

Chapter Twenty~Two

Bev waited for Dag Flanigan to show up at the inn to arrest her, look for the grannies, or even just to rest his head for the night. But after a week spent on tenterhooks, Bev finally exhaled a little. It seemed they'd gotten away with the impossible.

Of course, the town was rife with rumors and gossip about what had happened and where Flanigan had gone. Everyone seemed to have their own story, but the one Bev liked the most came from Allen via his sugar merchant.

"Yeah, he says that Flanigan's down south, still looking for that dragon flying in the sky," he said. "Tearing up the coast in search of it."

"I doubt that," Vicky said, sitting next to Allen.

She'd taken to helping him bring the pastries by in the morning, and Bev was pleased to see they were working so well together.

"I'm telling you, my sugar merchant has a wide area. He said Flanigan was on a tear headed toward the coast," Allen said. "Do you think dragons can fly that far? Or maybe it was a wyvern?"

"Could've just been a really large bat," Bev said, earning a snort from Vicky.

"I've got to get to work," Vicky said, rising and pecking Allen on the cheek. "See you this afternoon?"

"Can't wait," Allen said, squeezing her hand.

"What's this afternoon?" Bev asked as Vicky walked out the door.

"The start of our wedding planning," he said, sounding a bit less enthused than he had a moment before. "Vicky wants me *intimately involved*, she says, since it's *our day*. I'd rather just bake us a cake and leave the rest of it to her, but she's insistent."

"So I've heard," Bev said. "Do you two have a date in mind?"

"Two months from yesterday," Allen said. "I thought I might see if that cleric is still around. What was his name?"

"Wallace?" Bev smiled. "I can't say for sure, but you could write to Kaiser Tuckey and see if he knows where they went next. I'm sure he and Paul would like the coin."

Beasts and Baking

"Coin." Allen made a face. "This is going to cost me, isn't it? And Vicky doesn't want to involve her mother's family, even though they've got *loads* of money."

"I'm sure you'll manage," Bev said, opening her log book and making a note of the date. It wasn't as if she got too many advanced bookings, but it was good to keep a record of these things. "The inn will be yours for whatever guests you need."

"Hopefully, none," Allen said, rising. "But you know how weddings go."

"I've only been to one," Bev said. "I'm sure you and Vicky will make yours lovely." She paused, clearing her throat. "You should, however, probably let her know that the beautiful ring on her finger is actually a magical object. Just in case Mr. Flanigan makes another visit to town."

"Do you think she'll be mad at me?" Allen said. "We said no more secrets, but I don't know how she'd feel if she knew what it was."

"I think she's probably got a secret or two of her own," Bev said. "Might as well start your marriage off on the right foot by getting these things out in the open."

"Perhaps you're right," Allen said, before nodding to the two loaves on the counter. "Who are those for?"

"Ah, headed to Merv's today," Bev said. "I'd promised him a loaf of bread and to give him an update on everything. Since I'm finished with my spring cleaning, I thought it would be a good day for it."

Merv was doubly delighted to get loaves of bread as well as hear everything that had gone on in town. Bev gave him the full story, knowing her dear moleman friend wouldn't be crossing paths with any queen's soldiers anytime soon. He slathered slices of the bread with butter and munched down, licking his long claws as he finished.

"Shifters! I never would've imagined," he said. "And what brilliance to send the soldier Flanigan away to the east on a wild goose chase."

"Surprised it worked so well, myself," Bev said. "He's quite smart, that Flanigan. And—"

She paused, tapping her fingers on the cup and holding her tongue.

"And what, Bev?" Merv asked, his whiskers twitching.

"Well, it's just..." She sighed. She hadn't told anyone about her latest memory, not even Vellora, who'd probably been *in* it. "You know how I don't have a clue who I was before I showed up in Pigsend?"

He nodded.

"I've started to get *flashes* of things. Things that probably should remain forgotten." She stirred her large cup of tea with a spoon the size of her kitchen ladles. "The more I uncover, the more unnerved I become. I think I should just maintain my life as the innkeeper of the Weary Dragon, but…there's a part of me that wants to keep digging."

"What sort of flashes?" Merv asked.

"Well, it started with an amulet that was buried in my garden—an amulet that glowed again a few weeks later. I buried it in a thicket far away, but when I did, I uncovered the other piece to it. And with that came a *horrible* memory of what I believe to be a battle from the kingside perspective."

"Dear me."

"Then, during the solstice, I was talking with Vellora about a nasty battle she was a part of," Bev continued, "and I *remembered it*. Being there, fighting against soldiers with the same iron bangle that Dag Flanigan had on his person." She shivered. "I don't know if I should keep digging or just leave it be."

"What would you do if you uncovered who you were before Pigsend?" Merv asked, picking up his ball of yarn and starting to work.

"That's just it: I don't know. I feel…" She ran her finger along the rim. "If I find out who I was, and if it's someone who could make a difference in the world…" She let out a breath. "Who am I kidding? I was probably a scullery maid or something like that."

Merv made a noncommittal sound. "You've

always seemed to me a person touched by magic, Bev. What kind of magic, I haven't a clue. But magic. It's why that mischievous little laelaps is so loyal to you—they only bond with magical users."

Bev had known that, but she'd been ignoring that fact. "What should I do?"

"Well, if I were you..."

Bev leaned forward, waiting with bated breath.

"I would wake up every morning, do your chores, bake your bread, make dinner for the denizens of Pigsend, and continue living life as you are."

She sat back, a scowl on her face. "Very funny."

"Unless you find yourself some sort of superpowered wizard with the ability to dethrone the queen and undo all the damage she's done to the world."

"Doubtful."

"Then I wouldn't worry about it too much. You're Bev of Pigsend. Nothing more, nothing less. And if your past wants to come back to haunt you, then you can simply tell the ghost to go somewhere else."

Bev took a sip of her tea, unsure that sort of decision would be up to her. "Well, in any case, if I did have a bit of magic, it might make untangling these tricky situations a little easier. Maybe I could magick a person like Mayor Hendry and bend them to my will."

"Or steal her chairs," Merv said with a laugh.

She took another sip. "Wonder if we'll see any of the other soldiers again."

"As I recall, Karolina seemed fairly pleased to have seen the last of the town," Merv said. "And if Renault was to come back, everyone would recognize him, no? Puts a damper on his ability to fool people again."

"Unless he could magick a new face onto his own," Bev said.

"Now you're just talking silly," Merv said. "A new face. What kind of creature can do that?"

Bev sipped her tea. She didn't know, and she certainly didn't want to find out. "Suppose I should be getting back into town. I'm not sure Etheldra's forgiven me for not having dinner for her last night."

"But does she know what you did?"

"No one does. And I intend to keep it that way," Bev said, rising. "If you ever fancy a nice meal, you're welcome to join us at the inn. Be happy to give you a room, too, if you don't want to walk all the way back home."

"How about you come visit me again, and we'll just have a nice cuppa and catch up?" Merv asked.

"That sounds lovely, too," Bev said. "I'll see you soon, Merv."

Bev left Merv's feeling like she'd drunk her

weight in tea, but her soul was fulfilled. It was a shame Merv was a ways away, for she'd very much like to spend more time with him. Wim McKee never put much stock in holidays or breaks, but as much as Bev loved and cared for her beautiful inn, there was something to be said for a good friendship.

She meandered back into town, pondering what she might cook for dinner since it was probably going to be a small crowd, when she saw a familiar wagon parked out front of the Norrises's house.

"Holly! PJ!" Bev cheered, opening the door. "Well, aren't you two a sight for sore eyes?"

The teenager looked completely cured, with a healthy glow to his cheeks and a brightness in his eyes. His mother, too, seemed much less harried than the last time Bev had seen her. But the third person with them was the most surprising.

"Rita!" Bev exclaimed. "What in the world are you doing back in town? Thought you'd have moved on to your next place."

"My sister and cousin have set off north," she said. "But I had to make sure young PJ made it home safe and sound."

Bev glanced around the shop; there wasn't anyone except the Norrises and the two seamstresses. "Aren't you worried Flanigan will be back?"

"He's off chasing ghosts on the coastline," Rita

said. "And the kids gave us a good idea for the next time he comes sniffing too close to our affairs."

Bev wasn't sure it would work twice, but she was grateful it seemed to have this time.

"And now, thanks to that amulet, young PJ's magic is completely contained," Rita said.

Bev started. "Amulet?"

"Yes." Rita gestured to the boy, and he produced a small engraved amulet that was hanging around his neck.

Bev exhaled—it looked nothing like the amulet she had. "Well, thank goodness for that," she said, smiling at Holly. "How…was it?"

"It was terrifying," she said, earning a bashful look from PJ. "But also magnificent. They're majestic creatures. Proud to say my son is one of them."

"Do we have any idea how he came into his abilities?" Bev asked.

"Not yet, but it really doesn't matter. I'm sure all the magic in the ground helped whatever faint magic was in his blood," Rita said. "Hear that it's something of a common thing around Pigsend. People whose family didn't have a lick of magic suddenly sprouting all manner of abilities."

"So they say," Bev said. "You're off to join your sister and cousin, Rita?"

"Tomorrow morning." Her eyes sparkled. "Couldn't say no to one more night of your delicious cooking."

"You might have to fight with Etheldra for it," Bev said with a laugh. "Why don't we head back to the inn?"

~

Bev and Rita walked the short distance back to the inn in silence. Ramone and Horst were in the town square, measuring it and barking orders at each other. Hendry was overseeing them from the town hall, her fingernail tracing her blood-red lipstick. She gave Bev and Rita a once-over, but didn't say a word to them. Earl had not just Valta and Grant measuring and cutting wood near the schoolhouse, but the entire class of schoolchildren, with Bardoff hovering and presumably trying to make it into a math lesson.

"Seems like things are getting back to normal around here," Rita said.

"As normal as they ever get," Bev said with a smile. "Until the next calamity."

"I'm sure they'll call on you to solve it," Rita said. "I hear that's your specialty now."

As much as Bev didn't want to admit it, it was starting to look that way. Much like the pull to discover her own past, she couldn't help but become embroiled in the troubles of the town, in the hopes that she could help someone.

And it was *that* urge that scared Bev the most about finding out who she really was.

"What is it?" Rita asked.

"Just thinking," Bev said quietly. She licked her lips. "That amulet you gave PJ. Are there others like it?"

"What do you mean?"

"I've... As you heard, I'm not quite sure who I was before I showed up here," Bev said. "But I found... Well, I found an amulet. Pieces of one, at least. And I fear that it might've been." She swallowed. "Mine. But I don't know what it was used for or why it's in pieces. Was I the one to break it? Someone else? Is it the reason I don't remember who I was?" She sighed, sensing that she was rambling. "I had a flash of the war when I touched them together. And it glowed."

"There are many different kinds of amulets for many different purposes," Rita said.

"That's not helpful," Bev said with a shake of her head.

"Well, I doubt you'd find anything on the subject around here," Rita said, gesturing to the town. "Although your local librarian seems lovely, the queen made sure those kinds of books were destroyed. But if you were to find a place that hasn't been overtaken by the queen, you might find the answers you're looking for."

Bev started. Merv had mentioned such a place, just down the street, in fact.

Could Lower Pigsend be the key to unlocking the

mystery?

Rita nodded knowingly. "We did think there was something special about you, Bev. But we couldn't put our finger on it."

"I guess I was just wondering if it's worth it to find out more. Or if I should just let sleeping dogs lie." She rubbed the back of her short hair. "I'm afraid of what I'd do if I found out the truth."

"I don't think I believed you capable of fear," Rita said. "But my advice to you is to follow your heart. Memory or not, who you are hasn't changed. And if something is compelling you to find out more, I would follow that lead."

Bev nodded. "Tomorrow, perhaps. For today, I've got a date with a beef chuck roast and some parsnips, and one *very* hungry dragon shifter to feed."

"Oh, do you think you could add some carrots, too? I do love carrots and parsnips."

Bev continues her adventures in

MAGIC AND MOLEMEN

Weary Dragon Inn
BOOK FIVE

Acknowlegments

As always, first thanks goes to my husband for believing in me and taking the kids for a walk when I need time to exist without them. My village, too, stepped up in a big way as I got back on the horse after the birth of my second child. Speaking of, I'd like to thank him for demanding a six o'clock bedtime every night which allowed me to write the bulk of this book while he snoozed beside me. You're a rock star, little dude.

Thanks also go to my MI(L)F discord gals, for helping to push me along during this difficult time, and to Chelsea, Danielle Fine, and Lisa Henson for all the help.

Also By the Author

The Princess Vigilante Series

Brynna has been protecting her kingdom as a masked vigilante until one night, she's captured by the king's guards. Instead of arresting her, the captain tells her that her father and brother have been assassinated and she must hang up her mask and become queen.

The Princess Vigilante series is a four-book young adult epic fantasy series, perfect for fans of Throne of Glass and Graceling.

The Seod Croí Chronicles

After her father's murder, princess Ayla is set to take the throne — but to succeed, she needs the magical stone her evil stepmother stole. Fortunately, wizard apprentice Cade and knight Ward are both eager to win Ayla's favor.

A Quest of Blood and Stone is the first book in the *Seod Croí* chronicles and is available now in eBook, paperback, and hardcover.

Also By the Author

The Madion War Trilogy

He's a prince, she's a pilot, they're at war. But when they are marooned on a deserted island hundreds of miles from either nation, they must set aside their differences and work together if they want to survive.

The Madion War Trilogy is a fantasy romance available now in eBook, Paperback, and Hardcover.

empath

Lauren Dailey is in break-up hell, but if you ask her she's doing just great. She hears a mysterious voice promising an easy escape from her problems and finds herself in a brand new world where she has the power to feel what others are feeling. Just one problem—there's a dragon in the mountains that happens to eat Empaths. And it might be the source of the mysterious voice tempting her deeper into her own darkness.

Empath is a stand-alone fantasy that is available now in eBook, Paperback, and Hardcover.

About the Author

S. Usher Evans was born and raised in Pensacola, Florida. After a decade of fighting bureaucratic battles as an IT consultant in Washington, DC, she suffered a massive quarter-life-crisis. She found fighting dragons was more fun than writing policy, so she moved back to Pensacola to write books full-time. She currently resides there with her husband and kids, and frequently can be found plotting on the beach.

Visit S. Usher Evans online at:
http://www.susherevans.com/

Milton Keynes UK
Ingram Content Group UK Ltd.
UKHW022023151024
449742UK00015BA/147/J

9 781945 438707